Overture

her passion, his rules

Forbidden fruit never tasted this sweet...

> *"Swoon-worthy, forbidden, and sexy, Liam North is my new obsession."*
>
> – New York Times bestselling author Claire Contreras

The world knows Samantha Brooks as the violin prodigy. She guards her secret truth—the desire she harbors for her guardian.

Liam North got custody of her six years ago. She's all grown up now, but he still treats her like a child. No matter how much he wants her.

No matter how bad he aches for one taste.

Her sweet overtures break down the ex-soldier's defenses, but there's more at stake than her body. Every touch, every kiss, every night. The closer she gets, the more exposed his darkest secret. She's one step away from finding out what happened the night she lost her family.

One step away from leaving him forever.

CHAPTER ONE

Beethoven would count out exactly sixty coffee beans each time he had a cup.

SAMANTHA

THE WHIR OF the espresso machine lures me downstairs.

I'm not naturally an early riser, especially on a Saturday, but Liam always waits for me. The food could get cold, but he'd still be there, with his newspaper and his endless patience and his deep green eyes.

He gives me a small nod in greeting.

Only the sound of foaming milk breaks the morning quiet. There's avocado toast with walnut oil and fresh lemon juice at my place. On the other side of the table, scrambled egg whites and steamed broccoli. A ritual we've shared for the past six years…

And it's going to end in a matter of weeks when I graduate high school.

When I turn eighteen. When I leave for the

music tour that will take me around the country and across the globe… away from the man I've come to need more than I should.

"The interviewer from *Classical Notes* should be here at noon," he says, handing me a steaming mug with Earl Grey and lavender and a liberal splash of cream. He would never use anything as sweet and unnecessary as cream in his own drinks, but thankfully he's never controlled what I eat. He only controls everything else.

The reporter is doing a profile on me for the magazine. The famous child prodigy. *Ugh.* That's the last thing a seventeen-year-old girl wants to be called—a child.

I'm almost an adult now, but the label follows me around.

I take a fortifying sip of the hot liquid, closing my eyes against the burn. When I open them again, Liam looks at me with a strange expression. That's when I realize I let out a moan of pleasure. "Sounds good," I say a little too brightly, trying to cover my embarrassment.

He clears his throat and takes a seat at the head of the table. "Right. Well. I doubt the interview will take very long. I'll let him know you need to practice."

A strange thrill moves through me. Defiance?

Not exactly, but I feel energized all the same. He doesn't have to protect me anymore. And soon he won't have the right. The tour is going to change everything for me—and between us. I look forward to it as much as I dread it. "I do need to practice, but you don't have to rush the interview."

"Remember," he says as if I hadn't spoken. "You don't have to answer anything you don't like. If a question gets too personal, I'll step in."

My cheeks heat. Of course I know why he's being so protective. There were some disastrous interviews when I was six, seven, eight years old. Daddy didn't care to be in the room with me. Some of the questions would be inappropriate or downright aggressive. The classical music world is basically a viper's nest, and child prodigies are regarded with a mixture of awe and distrust.

And then there was the interviewer from a national newspaper. He had been ushered into the drawing room and left alone with me for thirty uncomfortable minutes, where he coaxed me to sit on his lap and nuzzled my neck. Daddy's aide found me crying in a closet hours later.

All of that is in the past. I'm no longer a scared little girl.

I shrug as if it doesn't bother me. "These

classical music reporters ask the same questions. Who's my favorite composer? Who do I want to play with in the future?"

Liam's stern expression doesn't waver. No doubt he remembers how I had trembled before the first interview, shortly after he got custody of me. I'd brokenly shared the story with him. At the time I was too afraid that he would give me away if I didn't tell the truth, to make anything up. So I told him about the reporter who held me on his lap. From that moment on I never did an interview alone. Liam is always there, always protecting me.

"Who *do* you want to play with?" he asks, his tone mild. As if he hasn't heard me wax poetic about my favorite violinists and maestros for years.

"I should say Harry March." He's the celebrity tenor headlining the tour. The rest of us have notoriety only in the classical music world. Harry March, with his crossover pop songs and playboy lifestyle, is basically a household name.

"You should say whatever's the truth," Liam counters.

"Well, I *am* excited about the tour." And I'm aware that the only reason I got the soloist spot is because the famous solo cellist on the Billboard

Top 100 was Harry March's lover—until their dramatic breakup that was covered by TMZ. "It's an incredible opportunity, especially considering I haven't been touring."

My cheeks flush because I hadn't meant to say that. It sounds like an accusation, even though it isn't. Well, not exactly.

Liam is the reason I haven't been touring.

"Because you wanted a well-rounded education," he says.

"Right." The word comes out hollow because it doesn't really matter what I think. Or at least it didn't matter for a long time. If Liam had said I wanted to be a circus clown, I would have gone along with it as a scared twelve-year-old girl. All I'd wanted was a place to call home.

Liam gave me that, which means more than he can ever know.

Soon I'm graduating from that well-rounded education. I'm going to turn eighteen. And then I'll leave on the tour, walking away from the only home I've ever known.

LIAM

THE DOORBELL RINGS at exactly noon. I like punctuality, but I'd like it even better if members of the press never spoke to Samantha Brooks again. I've limited their access to her greatly—maybe even to her detriment, considering press helps her get concert invitations and recording contracts.

I never planned to have children, and at the age of twenty-eight I had hardly been in a position to be the father of a twelve-year-old girl. That's exactly what happened when a judge signed the papers giving me guardianship of Samantha. Her mother had been long gone. Her father had just died. Her brother had no interest in a sister he'd never known.

Somehow the two of us, complete and utter strangers, became a family.

The sweet strains of the violin follow me downstairs. She practices every day before school. Every day after school. Every weekend. It's become the dew that coats every part of my life, a fresh breath of daylight in a world of dark.

It's hard to believe that in only a few weeks the house will be silent. I steel my expression into remoteness. It isn't the stodgy old reporter's fault that I resent the tour that will take Samantha away from me—and the press that's naturally a part of it.

"Hello." A woman in a sleek suit gives me a

slow smile. "You must be Liam North."

My eyebrows rise. This isn't an aging gentleman with white hair and a plaid sweater vest. Maybe the magazine thought a woman would be able to connect better with Samantha. The thought gives me pause. Maybe she's been missing a female influence in her life.

Dating has been the last thing on my mind the past six years.

"That's me." I shake her hand. "I'm going to sit in on the interview."

She purses ruby-red lips. "Why?"

Already this interview is going differently than the last one. The older gentleman had spent more time reminiscing about meeting Fritz Kreisler to ask too many questions. When he remembered to do the actual interview, he asked the kinds of standard questions Samantha remembered at breakfast. What routine do you have to warm up? What's the hardest piece you've played?

The man hardly noticed that I was in the room except to send me a reproving glance when he asked about her schooling. Why not attend a performing arts school? Did she want to move to New York City or London where she could have more exposure to professional musicians?

"Because I'm her legal guardian," I say, not

bothering to hide the steel beneath the words.

"Does that mean she isn't allowed to speak her mind?"

Christ. I have half a mind to slam the door on this reporter's face. I don't trust her as far as I could throw her. If this were six years ago, I would do just that.

It could risk Samantha's involvement in the tour, though. She earned the right to do this. I may be her legal guardian, but not for much longer.

"It means it's my job to protect her from members of the press who are more interested in a juicy story than the privacy of an underage young woman." I keep my voice level, but there's no mistaking my meaning. If she tries to pull anything in front of Samantha, she's gone.

The reporter smiles. "I'll be on my best behavior then. And if I step out of line, maybe we can meet up after and you can teach me a lesson I won't forget."

I stare after her as she heads into the house, following the sound of the violin without knowing the way. That's how rusty I am at dating—that it takes me a second to realize she was flirting with me. I have a feeling it's more than flirting. An offer. She would be in my bed tonight if I wanted her.

So why don't I want her? She's a beautiful woman, there's no doubt. And it's not like I have an abundance of options spending my days here at the compound. I don't date any of my employees or anyone who lives in Kingston. It might lead to complications. Come to think of it, I'm in the middle of a dry spell that's pretty damn long.

I already know that I'm not going to take the pretty reporter up on her offer. It has something to do with the violinist she's here to interview. *Because I don't want anything to distract from my duties as her guardian.* At least that's what I tell myself.

Samantha's face in rapture as she takes the first sip of her hot tea flashes through my mind. I'm afraid my reasons for abstaining may be something far more base.

No, that can't be right. Samantha is my responsibility. I'm sixteen years older than her and in a position of power. I absolutely cannot think of the small moan she made.

My body reacted to the sound with instant carnal hunger.

I grit my teeth and follow the reporter to the music room because I'll be damned if I'm going to let this interview get out of hand. Something tells me this reporter is eager enough to push her luck. No one messes with Samantha Brooks—not even me.

CHAPTER TWO

A single violin is made from over seventy individual pieces of wood.

SAMANTHA

I CAN TELL from the moment the reporter steps into the room that everything will be different. She has hair so glossy and curled—I didn't know it could look that way outside of a magazine. Her eyebrows belong in some kind of YouTube tutorial. And she's dressed like we're in a New York City high-rise instead of a small-town ex-military compound. The house is large and expensive, with marble floors and crown molding—but it's clearly designed to hold men.

Lots of men. Everything large and solid. Very few women ever walk through these rooms. There are some women who work for North Security. My friend Laney's mom is on the Red Team, for example. They're rare. And when they do come around, they dress and act as tough as the men—tougher, because they *need* to be tougher to survive in what's still mostly a man's world. A housekeeping service comes once a week, but they wear uniforms and comfortable, sturdy tennis shoes.

Nothing like the blush heels she wears.

She gives me a warm smile. "You must be Samantha. I'm Kimberly Cox. Of course I've read all about you. And that sounded absolutely lovely. I can see why everyone loves you."

"Oh." My cheeks turn warm. "Thank you. I'm not sure everyone loves me."

"When I spoke with Harry March a couple weeks ago, he said he was dying to meet you."

A startled laugh bursts out of me, embarrassing because it's so inappropriate. She must be exaggerating. Maybe she wants some kind of reaction? A lot of girls have crushes on Harry March. A lot of boys, too. "Well, that's very kind of him. I'm really excited to meet him, too."

She pauses, glancing around the room. "So this is where the magic happens."

"I don't like much distraction," I say, feeling as if I have to make excuses for the bare walls. The room is large enough for a whole orchestra to play in, almost a full ballroom, but there's only me. A single chair, not even cushioned. A stand for sheet music and my phone.

Liam appears in the doorway behind her, looking stern and… strange, somehow. His eyes have turned almost olive, a haunting color. He must have noticed that Kimberly Cox is nothing like the other classical music journalists we've met. Does he like the way she looks? Of course he likes the way she looks.

She's beautiful, and his eyes work just fine.

He doesn't say anything, only leans back against the doorframe—watching. Probably watching her. He's already seen me. I'm not the one with flawless eyeliner and amazing calf muscles.

Something dark and a little green stirs in my center. Is this jealousy? Oh my God, I'm jealous of this woman and the way that Liam North must think of her. Sexually, that's how he must think of her. As a grown woman. Not a child.

"There's a speaker system," I say, nervous energy making me speak. I pull up my phone and play Schubert. "Der Erlkönig" streams in perfect, terrible angst from all corners of the room. "That's how I practice accompaniments."

She cocks her head, listening. "This piece was based on a poem, wasn't it?"

"A child was taken by a monster in the woods." The high-pitched notes are the child's cries, and in response the father replies in low, placating reassurance.

It turns out to be an empty promise. The poem doesn't end happily. I press the Pause button on the app to stop the music. Silence reverberates in the room.

"Is there somewhere we can sit and talk?" Kimberly asks, glancing around at the empty room, where there are no other chairs except mine.

"My office," Liam says, striding between us and pushing open the door that separates the two rooms. His office is just as large as the music room, with a sitting area in front of gleaming walnut bookcases.

I take one of the armchairs while Kimberly takes the other.

Liam starts to close the doors, with him inside.

The reporter clears her throat. "Actually I was hoping to have a moment alone to interview Ms. Brooks. I know you're concerned about her, but she seems more than capable of speaking for herself."

A shadow passes over Liam's green eyes, turning them moss. "I made it clear that the answer to that is no. If you don't follow the rules, you'll have to leave."

Kimberly doesn't look surprised or taken aback by his hard tone. "Don't you think Samantha can make that decision? There will be lots of interviews on the tour, and you won't be there, will you?"

My stomach clenches because she's right. For so long I've done my best to be the good, obedient girl. *If you don't follow the rules, you'll have to leave.* That's been my greatest fear. Except I did follow the rules, all of them, and I'm still going to graduate and turn eighteen.

I still have to leave.

"I'll do it," I say, my voice soft.

Liam turns to me. "No, Samantha. She doesn't get to dictate what happens in this house."

No, I think, *only you get to do that.* "I'll think of it like practice," I say instead. "There will be lots of press stops on the tour, and I should be able to do this."

He frowns, and I think for a moment he might refuse. "I'll be right outside," he says, his voice dark. There's no question that I could have this woman off the property. The part of me that's small and jealous wants her gone, where Liam can't see her. Where he can't get turned on and think about sex and maybe even ask her out on a date.

The bigger part of me knows that she has nothing to do with it. There are beautiful women all over the world, and Liam North has no doubt dated many of them. He's always been careful to keep that part of his life hidden from me, part of his iron control and discipline, but that doesn't mean he's a monk. Does it?

I'm desperate to know something, *anything* about Liam's sex life.

Kimberly gives me a rueful smile as the door closes behind him. "I don't think I made a new friend with him. He sounded pretty strict about staying in the room with you."

"He's just protective," I say, feeling defensive of him, even though it would probably be better if she thinks he's an asshole. "You never really know what you're getting with reporters."

For example, sometimes they show up thirty years younger than you think.

She leans closer and gives me a conspiratorial smile. "All the more reason for him to be gone while we talk about your personal life."

"Oh." I blink, trying to make sense of her words. "I thought you… well, I thought you'd ask me about my favorite composer and who I want to work with."

"I'm assuming your favorite composer hasn't changed from the interview you did for BBC last year. As for who you want to work with, you should probably say Harry March even if that's not true."

A huff of laughter escapes me. "Okay, so what do you want to ask me?"

"My readers want to know the person behind the violin. They already know they're going to get your best when they buy a ticket. They want to know something they can't see onstage. What do you love about your best friend? Who's the last boy you kissed?"

Unease moves inside me. "I'm not dating anyone."

"Oh, come now," she says, coaxing. "There must be someone you're interested in. I know that you attend St. Agnes. That must give you even more opportunity to meet boys than if you only had tutors."

There is someone I'm interested in, but it's wholly inappropriate. Wrong on every level. Completely forbidden. I barely even let myself think it, but Liam is the only person that comes to mind when I dream about kissing or sex. "It's really just me and my violin," I say, trying to sound breezy.

I think that's how a woman of the world should sound. Someone who doesn't have a crush on the man who's been her guardian for the past six years. That crush feels painfully childish with this woman sitting in front of me, everything about her sexy and grown-up.

Thankfully she moves on to asking about friends and about school. Safe questions.

When she's done, she closes her notebook with a brusque *snap*. "Thank you so much for talking with me, Samantha. I appreciate your time and your candor."

My gaze hits the floor because I wasn't completely honest. It's not that I feel guilty about that exactly. I don't owe a random reporter my deepest secrets. But I do feel guilty about having the secret, about having a crush on the man who's only ever protected me.

That man waits in the hallway when Kimberly opens the door. "Just the person I wanted to see," she says. "The rest of my questions are for you."

CHAPTER THREE

The smallest violin comes in size 1/64th,
perfect for children aged two and three.

LIAM

CHRIST.

Samantha stands behind the reporter, her eyes wide with curiosity. And something else. Betrayal? "Questions for me?" I ask, keeping my expression blank. I sure as hell hope she isn't coming on to me with my ward in the same room.

Kimberly gives me a wry smile. "Part of my interview process. I like to speak to the important people in the musician's lives, get their perspectives."

I've been an important person in Samantha's life for the past six years. It wasn't a role I particularly wanted, but now that I'm here—the thought of her leaving makes me feel hollow. "I see."

"We can use your office," the reporter

prompts.

"Right," I say, hiding my reluctance. I don't want to discuss my feelings for Samantha with anyone. They cut too deep for words. I don't want to hinder her press opportunity. The way she stood up to me when she asked to speak to the reporter alone—it was a small thing, but it was new. God, she's going to be eighteen in a few weeks. I can support her independence… even if it kills me.

I stand aside to hold the door open for Samantha to leave. The last thing I need is her watching me while I talk about… what, exactly? My perspective, whatever that means. There's a dark undercurrent to my thoughts about her. Like the way I keep thinking of her expression as she moaned.

The betrayal in her wide brown eyes gets deeper as she passes by me on her way to the hallway. She's hurt because I'm kicking her out of the room. She'd be hurt a lot more if she knew these thoughts I have about her. That's why I plan on tamping them down—way down.

I close the door and glare at a knot in the wood. *Get your shit together, North.*

I've done some limited press for my company, making formal comments on the security for a high-profile client when it's required. More than that, I'm on conference calls with some of the highest-ranking politicians in the country. Nothing rattles me.

The look of betrayal in Samantha's eyes—that rattles me.

I don't join the reporter at the armchairs. Instead I take a seat behind my desk, leaving her to sit on the other side. "Your questions?" I ask, my tone brusque.

She sits down in a businesslike manner. "Thanks for taking the time, Mr. North. I understand that you've had custody of Samantha Brooks for six years."

"That's right."

"How is it that you became her guardian?"

"Her father passed away in—"

"Of course, the death of Ambassador Brooks is a matter of public record. I'm referring to the fact that you aren't related to Samantha through either blood or marriage."

The question hits me like a sledgehammer. I should have seen it coming. Years of military strategy should have prepared me for this, but I'm blindsided. For six years no one has asked me this question beyond the perfunctory reason that her father died. Her school, the society that awarded her a grant. I suppose it's alarming that someone could so easily take custody of a child that isn't theirs. A well-placed donation to a cause and a back-room deal with lawyers.

That's all it took to make Samantha mine.

She knows we're not related, but she thinks I was friends with her father. I could use that line with the reporter, but it sounds like she's done her homework.

How deep has she been digging?

"I knew her father," I say, choosing my words with care. I didn't know him as a friend, but I knew who he was. And I knew everything about him. "He passed without someone to care for her. I felt it was my civic responsibility to step in."

"Civic responsibility," the reporter repeats, sounding skeptical.

"That's right."

"The demands of raising a child prodigy are not ordinary. She has a famous violinist in his own right living nearby—you covered his expenses and pay a generous salary so she can meet him once a week. You deal with press interviews." She gives a little smile. "Like this one."

"It's no problem." This press interview is becoming a big problem.

From the smile playing at her lips, she knows it. "It's interesting that you were unmarried and had no children of your own when you decided to take on this civic responsibility. Had you met Samantha before you became her guardian?"

The question dances perilously close to, *Had you met Samantha's father before you became her guardian?* I don't mind lying to protect Samantha's privacy, but that might make things worse. It would be possible to confirm that there's no record of her father and me ever being in the same room together. How much does she know?

I stand up and face the window, which overlooks acres of North property.

"We hadn't met," I say without turning.

She was a twelve-year-old with messy brown hair and lost brown eyes. I had been completely out of my depth. It's a wonder she's turned out as smart and self-sufficient as she has, but I don't kid myself. She was mostly grown-up at age twelve.

Terrified and alone, yes. But she already knew how to survive—she'd learned that out of necessity.

Kimberly appears beside me, the sunlight bright on her pale skin. This is the kind of woman I should take to bed. The kind of woman that should make my cock hard. It's wrong, it's so fucking wrong, that all I can think about is Samantha's moan.

"That's interesting," Kimberly says, her voice low, as if she can see inside me. What would happen if she knew the truth? If she printed the truth in an article? "That the court couldn't find someone else to care for her. That they trusted you when you didn't even know her."

"The world is a stark place," I say.

There aren't always people who care about kids. My brothers and I learned that early. Samantha deserves more than that. She deserves all the safety and comfort I can find.

She deserves the truth too, but she's not getting that.

Kimberly turns so that her body is between mine and the window. She faces me, her breasts brushing my chest through our clothes. "I think you have secrets, Mr. North."

I'm not sure she's even aware of it, the choice she's giving me. I can kiss her. I can fuck this woman right now, and it will be enough to throw her off the scent. She may not realize it, but it's there, shining in her eyes. She wants oblivion, and my body can give it to her.

Am I willing to do that to protect Samantha's privacy? Hell yes.

Don't be so fucking noble, North. You're not protecting Samantha. You're protecting yourself.

And it wouldn't exactly be a hardship to have sex with a beautiful woman. Even if she's not the one I want. Kimberly's body sways toward me, sensing my deliberation. I catch her and keep her close, feeling her warmth. Why does she do nothing for me? No woman has done it for me. Maybe it's more than a dry spell.

Maybe I've been fundamentally broken.

Except that seeing Samantha makes my blood run hot.

That's when I decide to do it—I need to fuck this woman if only to prove that I can. If only to prove that Samantha is safe from my baser desires. I've always known I'm a fucked-up son of a bitch. That's why I picked a profession that could get me killed any minute. Someone has to do the job. Might as well be me.

Then Samantha changed everything. For the first time I actually wanted to stay alive.

I never would have shackled a woman to me. Never would have had children of my own, but Samantha… she's in a different category. The judge granted her custody to me, but from the moment he signed that piece of paper, I belonged to her.

My head lowers. I'm determined to exorcise my sexual demons with this woman who clearly wants this, who can handle it and walk away unscathed. Our lips meet. Every muscle in my body remains as hard and cold as marble. Desperation courses through my veins. How can I keep Samantha safe from this? From me?

An image of Samantha's face flashes through my head, her eyes closed in ecstasy, a low sound of pleasure vibrating through her throat. My eyes are closed, too. That's all I can see. I grasp the jaw of the woman I'm holding, then slide my hand to her neck. My other hand slides back to clench in her hair—something is wrong, this isn't what her hair would feel like. I pull hard enough that she makes a soft sound of protest.

My eyes snap open. What the hell am I doing?

I take a step away from the woman. She deserves more than a man who's imagining someone else. And Samantha deserves more than a guardian who thinks about her while fucking.

Kimberly's breathing hard. Her hand goes to her throat, where the skin is still red from my grip. "I knew it would be intense with you. But that was—"

"A mistake," I say, trying to soften my voice. Failing. I'm hard all over and nothing that happens in this room can fix that. "I shouldn't have kissed you."

In fact I really didn't kiss her. Our lips were a millimeter apart before I stopped. That's how close I came to finally finding relief, and all I feel is betrayal to Samantha.

The sensual haze slowly lifts from the reporter's eyes, replaced with that shrewd journalistic instinct I should never have let into this house. "Because you're seeing someone else?"

"Does it matter?"

"It might matter, if it's something worth writing about."

My eyes narrow. "You have an accusation? Come out and say it, Ms. Cox."

"I'm a journalist. I only have questions."

"I shouldn't have kissed you because you're here to do a story on Samantha Brooks, the prodigy, the soloist, who has incomparable talent and a hell of a bright future. You're not here to take your clothes off for me. Unless that's a perk that comes from *Classical Notes Magazine* now."

She flinches, which makes me a true bastard. She's done nothing wrong except be damn good at her job. It's the only way I can get her to back off the damn story.

There is no story.

Nothing has ever happened between me and Samantha, and that can't change. No matter how badly I want her. No matter how hard I ache for just one taste.

CHAPTER FOUR

String players, like violinists, tend to have larger brains. This is due in part to the complex motor skills and reasoning required to play the instrument.

SAMANTHA

THE STRING VIBRATES on a C sharp, the note echoing in the chamber after my bow lifts.

Silence descends in slow degrees. I could be turning the page to my sheet music or tightening a string. I could be doing any number of things to continue practice, instead of sitting with my violin across my lap, the bow clutched artlessly in my fist. I have lived a thousand lives in the dramatic rise of a musical piece, feeling the intensity grow, the complexity develop. This moment in my life should have been marked by an entire orchestra, bodies moving in harmony, instruments an extension of bone and flesh.

Instead there's only a curious quiet, so rare and therefore precious.

I feel the answering stillness in the room next

door. He could be shifting pieces of paper, noiseless and precise. He could be examining numbers and tactical formations on the flat privacy screen, but I know he's noticing the lack of music. We're connected enough that I can tell he's wondering what I'm doing.

I'm wondering the same thing.

Booted footsteps cross the gleaming parquet floor. Every aspect of this room has been designed to enhance sound, and it turns his approach into a military drum. He appears in the archway. The doors remain open every afternoon, even though my practice must disturb his work. Liam North takes his responsibilities seriously.

And I'm his responsibility.

"What's wrong?" he asks, crouching in front of me, taking in every aspect of my body with an impersonal evergreen glance. This is the way he corrects my position—no slouching, no leaning. He treats violin practice like a drill, and I am his soldier. I must do it right, must do it again, do you want to give up? No, sir.

Mostly, mostly, I love this about him. Today I don't.

What's wrong? This crush on him. It's wrong and taboo and completely unstoppable. "I don't feel good," I say, which isn't entirely a lie. I don't feel good, but I don't feel bad either. Instead I feel… enervated. There hasn't been room in my life for feelings before. Only music.

He studies me with the same impassive expression he would give a map. Around this corner and aha, there, through that mountain pass. Something he must traverse. "Since when?"

Since Kimberly Cox came to the house.

Since he kissed her in his office while I watched through a crack in the door. Though it would be more accurate to say she kissed him.

She stalked him through the house like a tiger over the plains.

And I followed her like a house cat, clumsy, copying.

She pressed her body against his. I heard his surprised inhale of breath, so quiet, so quiet. Heard the sound that came low in her throat. Her whole body moved in some purely feminine way, like water, so fluid. And he was a rock, solid and hard. Her hand reached between them, and he became somehow more still.

Until he grasped her wrist and pushed her away.

Something became warm inside me. Warm and new. Seventeen years old means I know what sex is about but I've never seen it, not that close, not with a man I looked up to like a father. Well, not exactly a father.

He may have legal custody of me, but I've never quite seen him as a father.

Something flashes through Liam's dark eyes. Worry? "Is it the tour?"

"No, of course not. I'm ready for the tour." Though *ready* isn't exactly the word I would use to describe myself. Terrified and breathless, maybe. The interview also drove home how soon I'll leave for the tour. Three months from now I'll walk out these doors.

Three months from now everything will change.

Liam puts his hand on my forehead, the contact so sudden I make a squeak of surprise. "No fever," he mutters, more to himself than to me. "Should I call Dr. Foster?"

"It's probably nothing," I say quickly, besieged by an image of the doctor making a house call. *Wet,* he would announce after an examination. *And flushed. And clenching her thighs every time you look at her. It's an acute case of lust, I'm afraid. Only one thing can cure it.*

I can understand Liam's surprise. When's the last time I caught a cold?

Maybe never.

In this household bodies are treated like one of the well-oiled guns in his cabinet. Organic vegetables and grass-fed beef. We sleep on a schedule designed for optimum performance. There's no entry in the procedure for *Samantha has a crush on Liam North, the man who's taken care of her for the last six years.*

"Rest," he says, nodding his head, decisive. "You'll take the rest of the day off."

"I'm sure I'll feel better tomorrow." Maybe once I've hidden under the covers, touching myself and pretending it's him, making myself come about a thousand times.

His brows draw together. It's a strange look on him. It takes me a minute to place it—uncertainty. He's never looked uncertain before. "Maybe I *should* call the doctor."

"God. No. Please."

That only makes his expression more severe. "Samantha. Are you sure?"

He doesn't wait for an answer. Two fingers tilt my chin up. His other hand holds my face up for his focus. His thumb brushes my eyebrow. My cheek. My jaw. All entirely ordinary places on a body, somehow lit by a thousand lights. There's no reason a man can't touch a young woman he considers his daughter, when he's worried that she's sick. It doesn't mean he wants to have sex with her, never that.

Except he looks a little shaken when he's done with his perusal, his eyes blinking as if surprised to find himself touching me, his throat working as he swallows. "You would tell me if something were wrong."

Not a question. It's a statement. "Yes."

I manage not to add *sir*, but only barely.

When I first moved here, I called him *sir* like the young recruits he trained. *Yes, sir. No, sir.* He inspires that kind of respect. The people from his company would raise their eyebrows when they heard me say it. *You run a tight ship,* they would say, sounding impressed and a little intimidated.

He told me not to, but it still slips out when I'm nervous.

You're not under my command, he muttered in a rare show of impatience, even though it feels like I am. Who else would I be under?

He's the one who gives me orders. I'm the one who obeys. We both know who's in charge.

It's like he can hear the unspoken *sir* anyway. His jaw tightens. "Go," he says.

He doesn't take a step back. Instead he watches while I bend to place my violin and bow in the case and close it. I stand up, but there's no room to stand or walk or breathe. He's filling every square inch of the room with his broad chest and dark eyes. Logically I know that I can walk around him, that he's waiting for me to do that, but somehow I'm standing here, one inch away from him, my small breasts almost brushing his chest when I breathe in and out.

There are foreign mercenaries and five-star generals who walk through these hallways. Large men. Muscled men, but none of them compare to Liam. There are a few sets of weights in the gym downstairs, but he doesn't use them. You practice the way you perform. That's what he taught me about the violin. It's the way he approaches his work, spending hours a day in the obstacle course that takes up a few acres in back.

Soldiers ten years younger than him can't keep up.

I know he's a large man, but it still feels impossible to look up far enough. When I meet his gaze, awareness sparks from him to me, every place on my body that's an inch away from his.

"Tomorrow," he says, his voice somehow lower. "You'll be yourself again tomorrow."

God, I want that to be true. I'm not sure who that is anymore. The obedient girl who practices her violin for hours every afternoon? Not exactly.

No matter how much he wants that to be true. Something is going to happen tonight. I'm not sure whether I'll become more myself—or less.

His scent suffuses my lungs, my mouth. There's hard, sterile soap and something earthy from working outside and the elusive musk that is Liam North. My lips part, as if to draw in more of him. His eyes darken to deep sage, though I'm not sure what it means.

My heart pounds in my chest, and I skip around him in a frantic bid for safety, a rabbit scampering away from a fox. The only reason I reach the door is because he lets me.

I race up the stairs even though no one's following.

Inside my room I lean against the door, eyes closed, panting like I ran a million miles to get here. I need to fix whatever's happening inside me. No more stopping in the middle of practice. No more imagining Liam losing control.

Whatever I do for the rest of the afternoon, it has to be the end.

CHAPTER FIVE

Bach and Handel were both blinded by the same ocular surgeon.

LIAM

I WATCH SAMANTHA flee up the stairs, looking scared enough to make me uncomfortable, lithe enough to make me ache. What the hell's going on with her today? *You'll be yourself again tomorrow.* I know that's not true. She won't ever be the timid little prodigy who landed on my doorstep, eyes wide behind her glasses, fingers impossibly nimble across the violin strings. She's still a genius with the instrument, but it's no longer a little girl who plays. It's a young woman, and I'm the one who can't go back to the way things were. I can't unsee the flush of arousal on her cheeks. *Fucking hell.*

I return to my desk and try to focus on the field reports from my agent.

After reading the same sentence five times, I have to push the reports aside.

Footsteps approach the office, and I tense, fighting the impulse to stand up and close the door. Josh is second-in-command for North Security. He also happens to be my brother. He's whistling and stomping and generally being a pain in my ass. The man can cross a South American jungle without disturbing a single tree frog, but he makes enough noise now to wake the dead. It's a harsh contrast to the sweet violin that usually fills the air.

"Problem?" I ask, raising a brow.

He pauses with an exaggerated tilt of his head. "Why is it so quiet?"

I glare at him, but it doesn't shut him up. "You're fired."

A hand to his heart, the dramatic bastard. "Where's our beautiful Disney princess making music and drawing all the little woodland creatures to the window?"

"It was *one* squirrel." One squirrel who pressed its little hands against the window every day for almost two months, listening to the music as if he could soak in its beauty.

Strange, feeling a kinship with a rodent, but there it was.

It's not an accident that Samantha's music room is right next to my study. The house has thirty thousand square feet. I could have put her anywhere, but I wanted her near me. I'm soaking up every goddamn second until she leaves for good.

Josh leans against the bookshelf and crosses one ankle over the other, the very picture of casual disinterest. I know my brother well enough to see right through his exterior. Unfortunately he also knows me well enough to see through mine. "What's up?"

"Maybe we shouldn't go out tonight."

"And skip Hassan's bachelor party? He would never forgive us. I would never forgive us either. We haven't had a break in weeks."

"She said she wasn't feeling well."

He frowns. "Samantha?"

"No fever. No cough. I could call Dr. Foster."

"Is it the tour?"

I make a growl. "Maybe. It's a hell of a lot of pressure. She wants us to think she's all grown-up, but an eighteen-year-old has a lot of growing up to do."

"We enlisted when we were eighteen," he says.

"And I'd take a battle zone over Carnegie Hall any day."

"She's more mature than you were at eighteen." He pauses. "Well, maybe not. You were an old fucking soul even as a kid. But so is she. You have that in common."

The press will be all over every conference. Press with interview questions about her father? Red carpets. Meet and greets with VIP guests who are heads of state and A-list actors. And then there's Harry March, the celebrity tenor headlining the tour, known for being volatile.

I hate that I can't protect her from any of it. "There's no way I can make her stop the tour. She's got her heart set on it."

"And you can never say no to Samantha."

That makes me scowl. "I said no to concerts if they interrupted school for the past six years. She deserves to make her own choices now."

"Not to mention she'll be eighteen by then."

My heart thumps against my chest in useless protest, but I make sure not to show any sign of it to my brother. Christ. I ignore the way my pulse thrums. It would be too easy to rise to the bait. Too easy to take the stairs two at a time and prove to myself that Samantha's still there, if only for a short time more. "Kiss my ass."

"You're really worried about her."

"Is there actually a reason why you're here, or do you just love to annoy me?"

"Annoying you is reason enough, in my opinion, but I do actually have something work related. The Red Team has gone dark." He stands almost at attention, as if we were both still in the navy.

That makes me pause. Three highly trained operatives could handle themselves in the frozen tundra. There were reasons they might go dark in order to maintain cover. "How long?"

"A week."

Of course. For all that Josh acts like he doesn't give a shit, he manages the daily operations of North Security with sharp intelligence.

He wouldn't have brought me this unless it was serious.

"What did their last report say?"

"I'm sending you the full file now, starting with the last entry, but it doesn't indicate a problem. We have their coordinates to the south of the Ural Mountains. No injuries or major setbacks."

"And the target?"

"Local intelligence indicated he might be hiding in the wilderness."

That left a lot of terrain to cover, but that's why I sent the Red Team. They're the best. Efficient. Skilled. And goddamn discreet, though that is really a job requirement here.

I stand and pace across the marble floor, something I do when I'm faced with a problem. It would be better if there were music being played by a world-class musician, but she's not feeling well. Why isn't she feeling well? *Focus, North.* "What's your read on the situation?" I ask because Josh has been with me through a hell of a lot of campaigns.

Those blue eyes are a little darker today. "It's a long time for what should have been a straightforward task, but they know the stakes."

The stakes, meaning detection by the local law enforcement agencies. Identify a traitor to the United States with enough survivalist tendencies to last ten years in the forest. All while remaining invisible to Russia's police and military. Straightforward? Yes, that's one way to describe it. Fucking dangerous, too. That's what we do.

"The Red Team is the best," I say, sitting down again. "We trust them. And if they went dark to stay off the grid, sending in another team could risk the entire operation."

Josh nods, looking about two percent relieved. He's a genius at operations, but it takes something different to be in command. The hard truth is that it takes heartlessness. I care about the men and women under me, but I still send them into the line of fire. I still risk their lives so we can all make a few bucks.

That's the cold and utterly honest reason why I'm the one sitting in this chair.

Neither of us mention that our brother Elijah leads the Red Team.

The three of us are related by blood, but it would be a stretch to call us a family after our upbringing. I'm the one who founded North Security, but I gave both my brothers a stake when they joined the company. Elijah insists on leading the Red Team, with its dangerous missions and its near-constant deployment.

"Oh, and Josh?" I say as he turns to leave. "Put the other men on standby."

I'm responsible for their lives, which means I'm also responsible for their deaths. It might be a bullet from the traitor or even local military taking umbrage to American mercenaries. It might be tomorrow or in five years, but whenever it happens, their blood will be on my hands.

CHAPTER SIX

A violinist burns about one hundred seventy calories per hour, almost twice as much as masturbating.

SAMANTHA

ZERO. THAT'S HOW many times I've stopped practice early.

I've never been someone overly interested in breaking the rules. A people pleaser, that's me. Especially if the person is a hard-ass. My dad wanted me to play the violin perfectly to impress his diplomat friends? I did that. He wanted me to clean our little apartment and cook dinner? I could make roast chicken with a side of green beans by the time I turned five. He wanted me to follow him around the world without uttering a single complaint. Done.

When he died, some part of the twelve-year-old girl thought it had to be my fault. My mother was from Indonesia. She met my father when he lived there—and she died a long time ago. My older brother had no interest in coming back to take care of me.

It was Liam North who stepped up to do that duty.

I knew, without anyone telling me, that I couldn't mess this up. We weren't even related by blood. He was friends with my father. Or as he'd said to the reporter, *I felt it was my civic responsibility to step in.* I was just a kid, but even kids understand basic math.

There was no one left on this earth to care about me.

I took every independent thought, even the tiniest shred of rebellion through my teenage years, and poured them into my music. Something safe.

Suddenly it's not enough.

I want to do something wild and crazy like go skinny dipping in the lake down the hill. I want to ride in fast cars and parachute out of a plane. I want to do something shocking.

My room looks the way I left it this morning, everything neat and orderly, my books in alphabetical order. Alphabetical order! I can't even blame that on my quasi-military surroundings. Liam North does not require this kind of precision from me. Well, he also doesn't really read anything that isn't a classified brief, but that's beside the point.

I pull out *A Concise History of Western Music* with its worn spine and shove it next to *The Rose That Grew from Concrete.*

And then clench my hands into fists to keep from moving it back.

"Such a rebel," I mutter to myself. "You're the actual worst at this." It's going to take a lot more than unalphabetized books to fix this ache inside me, and I can't even manage to do that much.

Rest, Liam told me.

He's right about a lot of things. Maybe he's right about this. I climb onto the cool pink sheets, hoping that a nap will suddenly make me content with this quiet little life.

Even though I know it won't.

Besides, I'm too wired to actually sleep. The white lace coverlet is both delicate and comfy. It's actually what I would have picked out for myself, except I didn't pick it out. I've been incapable of picking anything, of choosing anything, of deciding anything as part of some deep-seated fear that I'll be abandoned.

The coverlet, like everything else in my life, simply appeared.

And the person responsible for its appearance? Liam North.

I climb under the blanket and stare at the ceiling. My body feels overly warm, but it still feels good to be tucked into the blankets. The blankets *he* picked out for me.

It's really so wrong to think of him in a sexual way. He's my guardian, literally. Legally. And he has never done anything to make me think he sees *me* in a sexual way.

This is it. This is the answer.

I don't need to go skinny dipping in the lake down the hill. Thinking about Liam North in a sexual way is my fast car. My parachute out of a plane.

My eyes squeeze shut.

That's all it takes to see Liam's stern expression, those fathomless green eyes and the glint of dark blond whiskers that are always there by late afternoon. And then there's the way he touched me. My forehead, sure, but it's more than he's done before. That broad palm on my sensitive skin.

My thighs press together. They want something between them, and I give them a pillow. Even the way I masturbate is small and timid, never making a sound, barely moving at all, but I can't change it now. I can't moan or throw back my head even for the sake of rebellion.

But I can push my hips against the pillow, rocking my whole body as I imagine Liam doing more than touching my forehead. He would trail his hand down my cheek, my neck, my shoulder.

Repressed. I'm so repressed it's hard to imagine more than that.

I make myself do it, make myself trail my hand down between my breasts, where it's warm and velvety soft, where I imagine Liam would know exactly how to touch me.

You're so beautiful, he would say. *Your breasts are perfect.*

Because Imaginary Liam wouldn't care about big breasts. He would like them small and soft with pale nipples. That would be the absolute perfect pair of breasts for him.

And he would probably do something obscene and rude. Like lick them.

My hips press against the pillow, almost pushing it down to the mattress, rocking and rocking. There's not anything sexy or graceful about what I'm doing. It's pure instinct. Pure need.

The beginning of a climax wraps itself around me. Claws sink into my skin. There's almost certain death, and I'm fighting, fighting, fighting for it with the pillow clenched hard.

"Oh fuck."

The words come soft enough someone else might not hear them. They're more exhalation of breath, the consonants a faint break in the sound. I have excellent hearing. Ridiculous, crazy good hearing that had me tuning instruments before I could ride a bike.

My eyes snap open, and there's Liam, standing there, frozen. Those green eyes locked on mine. His body clenched tight only three feet away from me. He doesn't come closer, but he doesn't leave.

Orgasm breaks me apart, and I cry out in surprise and denial and relief. "*Liam.*"

It goes on and on, the terrible pleasure of it. The wrenching embarrassment of coming while looking into the eyes of the man who raised me for the past six years.

My hips pump against the mattress, pulling out the last few pulses between my legs.

And then I'm lying there, wrapped tight around a pillow, unable to move, panting.

I've never seen Liam looking anything other than calm and cool and capable. He can handle anything with a command that's almost terrifying in its competency. Right now he looks at a loss.

His voice is low and rough. "We should talk about this."

I can't think of anything in the world I'd rather do less. "Or we could just…" I hate that I still somehow sound breathy and turned on. There are little quivers in my thighs. "Pretend this never happened?"

"Come downstairs when you're—"

The sentence hangs between us, leaving me to fill in the blank. *Come downstairs when you're done fucking yourself in the bed I bought for you. Come downstairs when you're done humiliating yourself.*

He gives a short nod, as if the unspoken answer is the right one.

Then he turns, an about-face appropriate to any military ceremony.

Alone in the room I have no choice but to face the mechanics of untangling myself. Unclenching my fists from the pillow. Pulling apart my legs. Acknowledging the dampness between my thighs.

"Please be a dream," I whisper, but my face is too hot. Burning up. This is real.

On shaky legs I stand up from the bed and cross to the bathroom, where I wash my hands. Then my face. Then brush my teeth. I'm going into battle downstairs, and apparently good hygiene is my armor.

Or maybe I'm just delaying the inevitable.

CHAPTER SEVEN

Harvard University found that early training in the violin improves memory.

LIAM

FUBAR. THAT'S MILITARY speak for fucked up beyond all recognition. I've seen a lot of situations where the term applies, but none as fucked up as this one. As seeing a sexy woman hump a goddamn pillow while moaning my name, her soulful brown eyes locked on mine. Jesus.

And the worst part, the truly terrible fucking part, is how my cock is iron hard.

It's like walking around with a goddamn club between my legs. It would be way too big and angry to put inside a woman right now, especially one as delicate, as innocent as Samantha Brooks. So it's a real good thing that it's never going to happen. We're not a regular man and woman. This isn't a casual fuck. This is a person I'm responsible for raising. My ward.

I press the heel of my hand against my cock, willing it to go down. For someone with a ridiculous amount of control over his body, I'm acting like a horny teenager who's just seen a pair of tits for the first time.

Samantha appears at the door of my office, her cheeks an adorable shade of pink.

"Have a seat," I tell her, wondering if I should have had this conversation in the living room or maybe the conservatory. Where do normal families talk about the birds and the bees? Then again, we're about the furthest fucking thing from a normal family.

She crosses her ankles and folds her hands together, the picture of a good little student. Even though her little cunt must still be soft from orgasm, the folds still damp with arousal. It would be so easy to make her climax again, already warm and set and ready for me.

I lean back against the desk, trying not to think about how those hands looked clutching the pillow. "First of all, I'm sorry for walking in on you. I was worried and didn't think… well, you have a right to privacy, and I want you to know that."

Her flush deepens to red. "Please, sir—"

"Liam. We've talked about this." At the beginning I didn't want her to call me *sir* because she shouldn't have to do that. Lately there's a different reason. Because of the way my cock jerks every time she says the word. God, she's almost begging. *Please, sir.* That's how she would sound if I spread her wide on her bed, tasting her little pussy.

She coughs. "Can we just… is there any way we can pretend that never happened?"

Christ. The memory of her sweet little body writhing on the bed is forever burned into my brain. I see it every time I close my eyes. I can't imagine that changing any time soon. "Look, I should have talked to you about sex a long time ago."

"What?" The word comes out as a squeak.

"It's part of my responsibility as your guardian." And it's not my responsibility to demonstrate any of this personally—not, not, not. I can't touch her, but I can make sure she's educated about it.

"I'm almost eighteen years old."

"Which is why I should have done this a long time ago. It isn't right that I let my own… discomfort get in the way of your sexual education. I hired tutors for math and science and history, but I neglected this subject entirely."

She looks dubious. "You're going to hire a sex tutor?"

The thought of teaching her what she needs to know makes my blood run fast and hot. I swallow around the knot in my throat. I would show her where to put her hands, her tongue; I would give her so much pleasure, until tears leaked down her cheeks. "I don't think that will be necessary, but you still should know some elementary facts before you—"

Before she does what? Has sex? Who the hell is she going to have sex with when the only people she comes into contact with are military bastards employed by North Security?

As soon as the thought comes into my head, it's all I can think about. What if she wants to have sex with someone who works for me? How will I keep from killing him? Where will I bury the body?

Then an even worse thought occurs to me. "You haven't already had sex, have you?"

She looks stricken. "No, sir."

I'm screwing this up. I don't know what normal families do, what a healthy, supportive conversation about sex would look like, but it probably isn't this. "I wouldn't be angry if the answer were yes, Samantha. It's your body. You get to make the decisions."

Of course I don't mention that if a man under my command took advantage of her, I would have some very inventive ways to teach him a lesson. Never mind that I've recently become obsessed with taking advantage of her myself. I haven't touched her—and that can't change. I can't kiss her or lick her or… bite her. God, I want to bite her.

Her uncertain expression makes her look so young. "I'm the one who should be apologizing. Doing that in the middle of the day… saying your name… thinking about you when I do that."

Hell. I have to stand and turn away from her to hide the massive, throbbing boner in my slacks. "You can do all those things. I just need to make sure you understand safe sex."

She makes a face. "Why?"

Because there will be plenty of boys who want to fuck her on her goddamn global tour, where she'll be both a celebrity and completely inexperienced. "Because you're going to walk out of this house in three months, and you need to know what's out there."

Something passes through her eyes—maybe grief. "I see."

"So," I say, my voice businesslike. "Sex."

"I know about condoms."

She knows about condoms. "You do?"

"The oldest known use of condoms dates back fifteen thousand years ago, on a cave painting in France."

Surprise comes out as a racking cough. "Where did you learn that?"

"A history book."

I stare at her, shocked that someone so incredibly intelligent, an actual genius by multiple measures, is this clueless about sex. It's my fault, of course. I'm the leader in this house. It was my job to make sure she knew about her body. About protection. "Here's what you need to know about condoms. They're absolutely mandatory. If you decide to have sex with someone—and it *is* your decision—you have to use a condom. Say it back to me, Samantha. I need to know you understand."

"Condoms are mandatory," she says obediently.

That's good, but it's not enough. How could it possibly be enough? How could it convey to her how many assholes were out there, waiting for the chance to take advantage of her?

Is this how fathers feel when they send their daughters into the world?

I'm not her father. Not even close. I can't imagine Ambassador Brooks having this conversation with his daughter, even if he had lived to have the chance. He wasn't exactly a concerned father. His daughter had been a little secretary in his house, given orders and expected to follow them.

Are you treating her any better, North?

"Samantha."

She blinks up at me, so damn trusting. I want her to look at me that way with my cock in her mouth, with her eyes watering. "Yes, sir?"

"Call me Liam."

A little cough that's the closest she comes to telling me no. "Is there anything else?"

Damned if this little violin prodigy doesn't know how to dismiss a hardened, experienced soldier. She sits there so fucking prim and so heartbreakingly pretty I don't know how to handle it. Maybe she is ready to go out into the world, to experience sex, to discover how much better a climax can be when given by someone else's hand, but I'm not ready for it. Not even close.

CHAPTER EIGHT

The Japanese word "karaoke" comes from a phrase meaning "empty orchestra."

SAMANTHA

FOUR YEARS OLD. Saint Petersburg. The teacher suggested that I be placed in the music program so that it would be easier for me to acclimate to the school. Daddy signed the paper because it wouldn't cost anything. The school provided an ancient basswood violin with a hard plastic case. A wrinkled instruction booklet showed how to place your fingers and introductory sheet music. I stayed up night after night working my fingers until they were raw.

That began my love affair with the violin.

Even when I'm not playing, the music lives inside me.

I'm still warm between my legs, my body ready for something that's never happened except in my imagination. I've made love with music a thousand times, but never with a man. Especially not the man who invades my thoughts every time I touch myself. He's invading my thoughts right now, those green eyes and stern mouth a hazy picture in my mind. Muscles bunching in his jaw as he thinks about what to say next.

Things like, *It isn't right that I let my own… discomfort get in the way of your sex education.* That's what he thinks of when it comes to me and sex—discomfort.

I run up the stairs, still feeling the strings against my finger pads, the powder in the air. The hard gaze of Liam North. The sensations should be different, the structure of a violin wholly apart from the tangle of feelings I have around the man. They blur together anyway, a physical symphony I play and play.

When I get to my room, Laney is there. She's been my best friend ever since I moved here. She holds a black long-sleeve sweater in one hand and a black floor-length skirt in the other. "Oh my God," she says on a moan. "You could work in a funeral home."

"Concert dress," I say, rueful. There are black skirts in velvet and cotton and silk. Mandatory for playing in an orchestra, and even once I started playing solo, I still follow the rules.

"What about if you have to go to a party?"

"After a concert?"

"Is music all you think about? Don't answer that."

Actually my mind is flush with other thoughts, far more illicit, after the most uncomfortable sex talk in the history of sex talks. "It doesn't matter what I wear. We're not going to meet guys."

"Aha!" She holds up a blouse with silk ruffles and no sleeves. I usually pair it with a black camisole underneath and a thin suit jacket over the top, the fabric stretchy enough so I can raise my arms and play violin. "This will be sexy in a prim librarian kind of way."

"Why am I trying to look sexy?"

"Because we're going to sneak out and go to a club tonight."

"Tonight?"

"This is for Cody. You can't say no."

A few weeks ago Cody confided that the new coach at Kingston High made him nervous. That's how he said it—made him nervous. We thought maybe he was one of those macho bastards who would hit someone if they didn't run laps fast enough. It took some coaxing on Laney's part to get Cody to reveal what he really meant.

That he got a little too close to the boys he was supposed to be coaching.

"How is going to a club going to help Cody?"

"Ohhh, and these will be great underneath."

I stare at the tiny scrap of black fabric she's wearing. Spandex. "Those are booty shorts. They go under my skirt so I don't accidentally flash five hundred people after Brahms's 'Sonata No. 3.'"

"We can pair them with some stockings I saw in your drawer. That flash of thigh is going to be the sexiest thing these boys have ever seen."

"They're basically underwear. Why do we have to go to a club to help Cody? Why can't we help in a library? Somewhere that we can wear regular clothes and go during the day?"

"Because this guy has incriminating evidence on Coach Price."

"And he's just going to give it to us?"

"That reminds me. Do you have five thousand dollars?"

"Oh my God."

"Look, don't freak out. People our age go to clubs all the time."

"I've never been inside one."

"Because Liam still acts like you're twelve years old and watches your every move."

In my mind I can see Liam's stern expression.

Say it back to me, Samantha. I need to know you understand. Imagine if I told him I wasn't a virgin. *I already know about condoms because I use them all the time.* Well, maybe not all the time. Once would be enough.

Would he have been shocked? Probably. He might have tried to lock me up in a tower and throw away the key. Or maybe he finally would have seen me as a woman. He wouldn't treat me like I was a little girl if I wasn't a virgin. Would he?

"Fine," I say, grabbing the clothes. "We can stop by the bank."

She follows me into the bathroom. "I've been working on cat eyeliner."

"A little privacy, please?"

That earns me an eye roll. "Okay, Ms. Concert Dress. I happen to know there's no privacy in those backstage rooms. And no marble floors either. So stop complaining."

Privacy? No. There's not enough room for that. And any rooms with doors are taken by people having hookups before the show. It would have been easy to lose my virginity to someone playing the tuba or even a conductor, but I never wanted that. Being a so-called child prodigy has made me weird enough. I would like my first time to happen an ordinary way—with a man who cares about me, preferably.

Condoms are mandatory. The words come back to me in a humiliated rush, my cheeks heating with the memory. I actually said that to Liam North. The words came out of my mouth when I was only a few feet away from him.

Not only that, but I told him about condoms appearing on cave paintings.

Awesome.

The first attempt at eye makeup turns me into a raccoon.

The second one isn't much better.

By the third attempt Laney achieves a somewhat smoky eye that tilts up at the side. I stare in the mirror, wondering how I look like a stranger even to myself. The ruffled silk blouse and black boy shorts look cute and sexy and completely un-Samantha-like. Maybe this is what it would feel like to be normal.

Laney stands back, looking pleased with herself. "You look so slutty right now."

That makes me laugh. "Thanks, I guess."

She's an unconventional fairy godmother, transforming me into someone who can go to the ball. Some people think that Cinderella was weak because she needed help. Those of us who've been orphaned, who've been alone, who've been smudged in cinders, we know the truth. We can be strong every day of every year. The hard part is leaving it behind for even a night.

LIAM

KNOCK KNOCK KNOCK.

I've definitely learned to knock every single time I want to speak to her. Even if I hear voices coming from inside the room—Samantha and Laney. The door is too thick to hear what they're saying, but they've been friends for a long time.

"Yes?" That's Laney, sounding playful and defiant like she usually does.

It makes me wonder if Samantha told her about me walking in on her. I'm not sure whether I hope she does or hope she doesn't.

She deserves to share something that's bothering her. On the other hand, it feels strangely good to have a dirty little secret with her. Too good.

"Can I talk to Samantha?" I say through the door. Normally I would have opened it by now. It's not like Samantha's humping a pillow at this exact moment. Except I can't bring myself to turn the knob. My fist tightens on the cool metal, but all I can see is small hands clenched on a white pillowcase.

"No," Samantha says, too loud and fast. "We're having girl talk. Very, very private girl talk."

Very, very private girl talk.

Then she *is* telling her friend about what happened this afternoon. My cheeks feel warm. Jesus. How long has it been since I actually blushed? Certainly not when I saw her hips fucking a pillow. All I felt was pure lust. Now I'm wondering what she's saying about me. *He's a fucking bastard who's barely hiding his erection when I'm around him.* No, she wouldn't talk like that. It's the truth, though.

"I'm heading out for the night. Call my cell if you need anything."

"Okay," she says through the door, her voice like a squeak.

Hell. "Leave her alone, North," I mutter to myself.

The rest of the men are already gathered downstairs, wearing clothes other than fatigues for a change, laughter bouncing off the walls. I meet Josh by the wet bar, where he's pouring himself a drink. He salutes me with a wry expression. "Thought I might not see you tonight. Figured you'd stay here and play nurse for the night."

"Fuck you."

Eyebrows go up. "Well, well. What crawled up your ass?"

Having to give a safe sex talk to the girl in my custody, a girl I'm responsible for. A girl I want to taste more than my next breath. "What are we doing tonight?" I ask, ignoring his question. "Because I already know it's not a strip club."

"Not when you threatened to kick my ass."

"Sorry, but the stink of desperation and coercion really messes with my hard-on."

"What about a girl who loves attention and dancing?" Josh says, challenging me. He likes fucking with me. And apparently, he also likes strippers.

"Are you really going to tell them apart?" I ask, my voice caustic. I can't keep my employees from visiting a strip club on their off time, but I'll be damned if I go with them.

"Or a college girl who's paying for tuition on tips?"

"What about all the girls turning in their take to a pimp at the end of the day? The ones kicked out of their homes? Underage? What about the ones who don't have a fucking choice?" I stop myself, breathing hard. Too late, I realize how much I gave away with my little speech. It's too painful to think about what could have happened to Samantha without someone to look after her. Her violin fame might have given her some protection—or it could have made her a greater target.

He gives me a hard look, but his voice is light. "Okay, we can have a good time without the chance of human trafficking. If you insist."

I wouldn't be okay with strippers on a regular day.

Today is not a regular day.

After having the sex talk with Samantha, I have no desire to watch men reduced to animals over a pair of tits. Especially when all I can see is Samantha's full lips forming my name, her eyes fluttering as she imagines me between her thighs.

"So what's the plan?" I say, forcing my tone to be casual.

Josh pulls out his phone and texts me. The message contains only a photo of an ordinary brown rock holding down a one-dollar bill. The prize. "Jeff's going to fly us over the desert," he says, referring to our resident pilot. "We each get a parachute and a bottle of water. First one to find the prize wins."

This is what happens when you put a bunch of over-muscled alpha men together. We have to compete to find out who's the best, even if one of us has to die trying.

I glance down at my gray button-down and black slacks that I wore for a night in the city. "You could have told me before I got dressed."

"There are a handful of not-quite-street-legal cars waiting for us at the rendezvous point. We'll take them into the city. Drinks. Dinner. More drinks."

Hassan joins us at the bar, throwing his arms over our shoulders. He's already buzzed, which is maybe not ideal for jumping into the desert. "Let's get this fucking party started," he says.

I raise my eyebrow at Josh, who sighs. We'll have to jump after Hassan and make sure he makes it to the rendezvous point. It wouldn't do to have him die the night before his wedding. His fiancée would be pissed, for one thing. And all those hors d'oeuvres would go to waste.

CHAPTER NINE

The Helicopter Quartet was written by controversial composer Karlheinz Stockhausen. It involves sending four members of a string quartet into the sky in four separate helicopters and having each musician play their individual part. Meanwhile, they are recorded and broadcasted into an auditorium where they are all played simultaneously for an audience. Stockhausen reportedly composed the piece after a series of unusual dreams involving helicopters and a swarm of bees.

LIAM

THE CALL COMES when I'm ten thousand feet above the ground. A small buzz in my pocket, which reminds me to zip my phone and wallet into the harness so I don't lose them on the way down. I glance at the screen. A notification that someone's at the south rear exit.

Someone's always coming and going at the compound. An overzealous security system monitors every single entry point. I'm anal enough to leave the notifications on even though I don't usually need to see who it is. Except right now almost everyone is on a job or in the chopper. I left two men at North Security, one on guard duty, one off. I don't expect trouble, but I'm a cautious man. Untrusting.

Which means there are very few people who could be leaving right now.

If I had to guess, it would be Cody in his beat-up truck that's older than him with a hundred and fifty thousand miles on it. He probably visited Laney and Samantha, playing Mario Kart in the game room. There are a few people in front of me to jump, so I swipe to pull up the secure app that streams the video cameras.

Sure enough, there's the white truck pulling to a stop.

The gate slides open, well-maintained and smooth. The truck pulls forward and disappears from view. Relief fills my chest, which is funny considering I'm about to jump out of the open side door of the chopper. This is an adrenaline jump. A good-time jump. A hundred times easier than having the sex talk with Samantha, pretending that I think of her as a daughter when I don't.

Hassan jumps, and the men cheer.

The next few guys go quickly. They're eager to get down on the ground so they can beat the groom-to-be. Either that or they're hungry. Probably both.

Josh glances back at me, a question in his eyes. We've been through enough close calls that he can feel the unease inside me without me having to say a word. He can feel it even before I do.

Why the fuck am I uneasy?

Everything I do at home, the training and the security, it's about precaution—not actual danger. That's for South America and the Middle East. That's for the fucking jungle that is Washington DC. In the hill country of Texas? This is my land. I shouldn't be worried about a damn thing.

I give Josh a terse nod. Whatever it is, it can wait.

He offers a salute, lacking his usual ironic twist.

When it comes to the command structure, we don't fuck around, not even on a bachelor party. He jumps, his movements as casual as stepping off a porch. The wind carries him sideways, so it looks like he's floating. In the next moment a deepening fog swallows him whole. My stomach clenches into knots, but it has nothing to do with the men who just jumped out of the helicopter.

"Your turn," comes a voice in my ear. The pilot.

"Sorry, Jeff. Looks like you're our designated driver."

"We're all driving once we get to the cars," he reminds me, his voice unnaturally clear as the wind buffets around me, pulling me toward the door even as it tries to shove me deeper into the belly of the chopper. "And I'd rather be behind the controls than jumping out."

I glance at my phone again, sliding the little circle on the video replay back. There's the white truck again. I can make out his silhouette, but only barely. It's brighter in the air than it was on land. Dusk already fell. I narrow my eyes at the video, watching as the truck pulls forward.

There. A movement, breaking the flat line of the seat beside him.

As if someone had been crouched low to hide from the cameras, bobbing up a second too early. Who the fuck is in the truck with him? I'm afraid I already know. My gut was legendary in the navy. It's not about a magical sixth sense. It's a culmination of all my tactical knowledge and hands-on experience. A million different data points coalesced into a single decision—safety or danger. Life or death.

"Hell," I say.

"What's wrong?"

"Take me back to the compound," I say, biting out the words. Except they're already gone.

Even at 150 knots it's going to take twenty minutes. They already have a head start, and there's only one place they would go, especially without telling me. Into the city.

To practice that safe sex you told her about, my mind says helpfully.

Jesus.

"Sir?" comes Jeff's voice. He wouldn't normally question an order, but this isn't exactly a mission. If I stay quiet another two seconds, he's going to turn the chopper around no matter what.

"Belay that," I say, my voice harsher than I intend. "Keep going."

"Yes, sir," he says, which is basically the same as asking what the fuck I'm thinking.

I honestly have no idea. Why the fuck is she going into the city right now? The answer is simple: to put the safe sex talk into action.

Which means she could be hooking up with some frat boy right now.

All I can see is red when I think of some asshole in a club thinking Samantha's an easy target. It would be easy to blame Laney for being a bad influence or Cody for helping her sneak out, but Samantha's a smart girl. She knows how dangerous the world can be. There's a fucking reason she isn't allowed to drive around without an escort.

But I haven't told her every single reason. That's on me.

Yeah, I'll take this jump, but I have no intention of tracking down a dollar bill.

"Tell the boys not to wait up for me," I say. That's the last thing I get out before I step off the helicopter floor. The wind holds me tight in its grasp, sucking the air out of my lungs. I'm twisted and turned, and I let my body drift through it.

Adrenaline surges through my veins, but I save it, save it, save it. That's for later, when I find Samantha somewhere in the city. And whatever fucker thinks he can put his hands on her.

SAMANTHA

BASS REVERBERATES THROUGH rusted metal and torn leather. The truck pulls to a slow stop around the corner from the club, hiding in the shadow of an abandoned warehouse.

"I don't like this," Cody says, gripping the steering wheel like he's forcing himself to keep it still. He looks about two seconds away from kicking the gear into drive and taking us home.

"Of course you don't like it," Laney says, fighting to open the door. It fights right back, struggling to keep her inside as if it's an extension of Cody's will. She gives it a kick with her black heels, and the door finally springs open with a bereaved grunt. "You don't like anything fun."

"We're only going for an hour," I say quickly before Cody can change his mind.

Cody lives with his father in an apartment in town. His father isn't around much, which is probably a good thing. Most nights he's in a bar starting a fight.

And spending the next day in lockup.

Laney's mother works for North Security. She's on the Red Team, the most active group of soldiers, so Laney stays on the compound more often than not. The three of us made up a strange little band of friends, despite our many differences. Like the fact that Cody has in-out privileges at the gates without needing a security escort. That comes from doing work after school on the compound. Ironic, since he's the only one of us who doesn't live there.

"Why did I agree to this?" Cody mutters, more to himself than to me. "Your parents probably know a hundred ways to kill someone. And they're definitely going to kill me."

"No, they're not, because they're not going to find out." Laney slams the door shut and then smiles sweetly through the dusty window, posing as if for a camera.

I hide a wince in the back seat. It's not a very well-kept secret that Cody has had a crush on Laney since the day they met. That's not exactly Laney's fault. She can't help the fact that he has a crush, but she does seem to take a certain delight in tormenting him.

"I'll make sure she's safe," I promise, stepping out into the cool night.

"Hell," Cody says, and I close the door against the ache in his voice. He wants to be the one escorting her into a nightclub like the line of couples behind a velvet rope. Not as part of a secret night out and definitely not as our designated driver.

"You're mean," I whisper as Laney links our arms together.

"Maybe," she says, sounding a little sad. "But this is for his own good."

"I still think we should tell him what we're doing."

"He would never have driven us here if he knew."

Laney tosses her hair back, marching right up to the bouncer, bypassing the line of people. "Hey, sweetheart. We're looking for a good time."

The man has arms the size of my head. He

looks intimidating, and considering I live in a sprawling complex that houses armed mercenaries, that's saying something. His dark gaze sweeps down Laney's body, leaving no doubt that he's weighing what he's seeing.

My impromptu blouse and short shorts might look sassy enough to get into a club, but her red dress is the star of the show.

"What's your name?" he asks.

"The name's Jennifer," she lies.

"Sure it is," he says, stepping aside to let us in. "I go on break in thirty."

Laney waves at him as we slip past.

"How are we going to find this guy?" I shout to be heard over the *thump thump thump.* Someone stamps my hand, and then I'm shoved into a sea of people.

Bodies move me back and forth, interchangeable, indistinguishable. My stomach clenches. I've never been around this many people at once. Strobe lights flash over the blinding white smile of a woman. The heavy-lidded eyes of a man. Writhing bodies that make plain the kind of sexual knowledge I could only pretend earlier, humping my pillow alone.

CHAPTER TEN

The word "music" comes from the word "muse" in Greek. The Muses were daughters to Zeus and Mnemosyne, and protected the arts, including writing, dance, and music.

SAMANTHA

THE FRONT LOOKS like a warehouse with a bar installed. Laney slips a wad of hundreds to a bouncer, and we wind up in the VIP section in the back.

Once we slip past the red velvet curtain, the scene changes completely. Deep leather couches create little islands for people to talk… or other, more physical activity. Raised sections of the floor surrounded by a metal railing put on a show.

"Women only," the bouncer says, nodding to the platform.

"Sweet," Laney says, grabbing my hand. "Let's dance."

I linger near the entrance, reluctant to be the center of attention. There are other women dancing, and Laney was right about one thing—

my impromptu outfit doesn't look out of place. "We're not here to dance," I say. Laney is crazy smart, but she's like a hummingbird, drifting from flower to flower, her body held in suspension only because of how fast she moves.

She snorts. "Yeah, sure. Let's stand at the door asking every person whether they're going to sell us incriminating photos. We're trying to appear normal, remember?"

That's enough to push me up the short steps to join the other women. I can be normal, damn it. I can do normal things like dance in front of a bunch of men I don't know in what basically amounts to my underwear... Acid rises in my throat. Oh God, I can't do this.

I've never heard the song that plays over the speakers, loud enough that the bass reverberates in my bones. That's just another sign that I'm *not* actually normal. I can name the composer in a handful of opening notes for most classical music, but I don't know what's popular on the radio right now.

A man reclines on the black leather, his skin a sharp contrast to the shadows, his gaze locked on mine. Most of the men are looking at the bodies in motion. He's looking at me—with amusement.

Panic wraps itself around my throat, and I

close my eyes against the strobe lights.

The darkness settles over me, and I can block out the dancing around me and the men surrounding us. It doesn't matter that I don't know the song. I know the beat. The notes. The rhythm. Music is a universal language, and it speaks through me now, moving my hips in time.

In the best moments I don't move the bow or the strings. It's they who move me the way they need. That's what happens now, a kind of perfect passivity. The bass takes hold of me. My body reacts to the overt sexuality of the lyrics, turning warm and then hot, molten by the time the track *thump thumps* its way to transition to a new song.

I open my eyes and realize that Laney's watching me, her eyes wide. And she's not the only one.

"I didn't know you could dance," she says, something like awe in her voice.

Heat rushes my cheeks. "I can't."

That makes her laugh, almost a euphoric sound, one that expresses the freedom that I feel in every breath after being caged for so long. "You should see yourself."

I can't help but grin back. "You're a maniac."

"Back atcha," she says, throwing her arms around me for a hug.

"I'm going to look around," I say as I squeeze

her back.

There is no one more loyal or caring than Laney, but she's already distracted by the music, shaking her booty with another woman when I duck beneath the railing.

I glimpse broad shoulders in the crowd, and my heart skips a beat.

It can't be Liam, of course. He doesn't know I sneaked off the property. He doesn't know what club I'm in or that we paid our way into the VIP section, but that doesn't stop the worry from bumping through my veins. Swallowing hard, I force myself to skirt the edges of the room, looking for someone who might be looking for me.

Laney is right about one thing—we can't stand at the door asking every person whether they're going to sell us incriminating photos. Only about half of the clubgoers are dancing.

The other half are standing around, looking sexy and faintly dangerous.

Then I glance up at a dark balcony. There are no dancing people up there. Only a single man wearing a black button-down shirt and dark jeans. I recognize him as the one who watched me dance before. He could be any one of the men come to pick up girls, but he surveys the club with a sense of proprietorship, as if he's above it all.

His dark gaze meets mine, and an eyebrow arches in challenge.

I feel my cheeks flush. Is this how I would react to anyone flirting with me? Except I have the sense that he isn't flirting. At least, not only that. There's a sense that he's waiting to see whether I'll react. Like maybe he's looking for the buyer to incriminating photos.

Circling the edge of the room I find a black spiral staircase with a thin metal railing. It leads me up to the balcony, where he remains with his forearms on the rail.

"What's your name?" this man asks.

"Samantha," I say before realizing that I could have made something up.

North Security is located in Kingston, Texas, a small town that had plenty of undeveloped land for Liam to purchase twenty years ago. There are endless hills for his obstacle courses as well as natural features like lakes and cliffs and even caves.

People in Kingston know the ex-military men who visit the security company. Sometimes they even know Samantha Brooks, the violinist who appears in newspaper articles.

We're in Austin right now, the city with a

sprawling college campus and state government buildings and a bubbling tech industry. There's no way anyone would know who I am. Except that he gives me a slight, knowing smile.

"Samantha. You look different than the pictures online." There's nothing but ordinary lust in his eyes as his gaze dips to my silk blouse and the flushed skin it reveals.

"You're the one with the photos?"

That same slight smile. "Let me get you a drink."

I narrow my eyes. I'm the one who's going to be giving him money tonight, not the other way around. "Are you the person I'm looking for or not?"

"You don't trust me?"

"Not as far as I could throw you."

He laughs. "Smart girl."

I glance back at the platform, but I can only see a flash of Laney's dark hair. She's clearly enjoying herself, and I have no desire to put a damper on that. Besides, I don't need her to make this exchange. I can do this and prove that I'm an adult. That I don't need Liam North. Knots tighten in my stomach, because he would be furious if he knew I was here right now.

Which is exactly why I need to do this. My

imagination may not stretch that far, but I need to solve my own problems. Maybe then I'll be able to move past this completely inappropriate and unrequited crush. Then I can move on to a quiet, boring life of endless practice, alone, alone, alone, playing the violin until my fingers fall off.

CHAPTER ELEVEN

Baritone Leonard Warren died onstage at the Met in 1960 just as he had finished singing Verdi's "Morir, Tremenda Cosi," which means "To Die, a Momentous Thing."

LIAM

ONCE I HIT the ground, it takes twenty minutes to get to the drop point.

A row of luxury cars stands at attention—an orange McLaren, a red Ferrari, a yellow Lamborghini. Hassan is already there, holding up a dollar bill and grinning at me. His smile slips when he sees my expression.

"Something happen, boss?"

He means did something happen with the Red Team or one of the other men. Something life or death. Samantha sneaking out at night doesn't qualify, even if it feels that way in the heavy beat in my chest. "No, but I'm going to head out before the rest of the guys make it. I'll catch up with you tonight."

He still looks concerned. "You sure?"

"Positive." I don't want to disrupt the bachelor party any more than I will by leaving early. More than that, I don't want any witnesses for what's going to happen next.

Mostly because I have no idea what's going to happen next. I'm a man who makes a plan and sticks to it. There are contingencies built in at every step. No surprises.

And somehow, somehow I'm fucking surprised.

I decide to take a rebuilt silver Rolls-Royce Phantom because it's the least ostentatious of the group, which isn't saying much. The keys are hidden under the back wheel in a little case I know to be fireproof and highly secure. Luckily I already know the combination—I study the shape of the back; 1956, the year this car was manufactured, though not the year it was sold.

That's what Josh would pick.

Sure enough, the case opens to a plain silver key.

I'm driving down the dirt road when Josh and another man make it over the crest, their silhouettes in my rearview mirror. Hassan will let them know that I've tapped out, and I have no doubt that they'll enjoy the evening on North Security's corporate credit card.

Cody answers the phone in two rings. There's a pause. Then, "Yes, sir?"

He's not officially under my command, not the way the ex-military men and women are on payroll. He does work for the company after school. Mostly he purchases supplies for the house and helps me build the training courses.

So there's no reason he needs to call me *sir*, but he does anyway.

I've always found it endearing.

Now I have to grit my teeth against the urge to swear at him.

"Where are you?" I ask instead.

A pause. "Sir?"

"I assume you're still with them. I know that even if you were stupid enough to sneak the girls off the compound, you would never leave them alone where anything could happen. Right, Cody?"

A longer pause this time, one I imagine he's going to break by blaming the girls for making him help them or try to play it off like it's no big deal. Stronger men than him have cried when I use this tone. *Give me the right answer or they'll never find the body,* that's what this tone means.

"No, sir," he says slowly, and I have to give him credit. He sounds resigned to his fate, but he isn't buckling. "I'm right here waiting for them, outside Club Melody."

"Don't move," I tell him before hanging up. "Not an inch."

He can follow an order, at the very least. He's parked on the other side of the street from the club. Laney's sitting on the back of his truck, legs dangling over. Both of them have a worried expression, which kicks my latent panic into high gear. I've been trying to reassure myself that teenagers go out at night all the damn time.

But the solemn expressions of Cody and Laney make me want to radio in every single team under my command and declare a fucking war.

"Where is she?"

Cody swallows. "Inside the club. At least I'm pretty sure."

"It's my fault," Laney says, putting her hand on his arm. "I'm the one who wanted to go out, who convinced Samantha to come with me. And she was right there. We were dancing in the back, the VIP section. She took a break. I thought she was going to get a drink or something."

"She's not old enough."

"I know." Laney wrings her hands together. "Cody called and told me you were coming, and I looked for her so we could meet you outside. But she wasn't by the bar or in the bathroom. I tried asking around, but people could barely hear me, and I don't know where she went."

The girl seems near tears, and Cody puts his arm around her shoulders, managing a glare at me—which really takes some balls, under the circumstances. "Take her back to the compound," I tell him, my voice hard. "You and I will have a talk when I get back."

His brows draw together. "But Samantha—"

"I'll find her and bring her myself."

CHAPTER TWELVE

In 800 BCE the first recovered piece of recorded music was found. It was written in cuneiform and was a religious hymn. It should be noted that cuneiform is not a type of musical notation.

SAMANTHA

THE MAN LEADS me to a back room in the club. I'm expecting a supply closet or a bathroom—something secret and genuinely illicit. This is an office, a little messy but clearly used by someone with authority. Framed vinyl records line the walls.

He reclines on a file cabinet, his posture relaxed.

"Do you work here?"

"You could say that. I also own the place."

I reach for my clutch, which contains the envelope. "Then why do you need money selling photographs of sleazy coaches?"

A low laugh. "How do you think we afford strobe lights around here? My business is information, and you want to buy information."

"Fine. Show me the video, and I'll give you the money."

He gives me a slow grin. "What's the hurry? I saw you dancing out there, sweetheart. Wouldn't mind getting to know you a little better."

I swallow hard. "Not interested."

The sound of a scuffle in the hallway catches my attention. The door slams open, revealing Liam North in sharp relief, his eyes a brilliant, burning emerald.

"Oh no," I whisper.

If Liam finds out what we're doing here, everything is going to be ruined. Luckily the man seems to know that as well as I do. He takes a step back as if he'd just been touching me, as if he's just been caught in the act. "Christ. You underage?"

"Out," Liam says, and the man gives him a nervous look before leaving.

I stare at Liam. "Oh my God. You followed me here?"

He stalks into the room. "That's what you're going to say right now? How about, I'm sorry I snuck out of the house at night and gave you a heart attack, Liam?"

Pretend you came here to make out with a guy.

"I'm not going to apologize."

A low growl fills the room. "You followed a man to a back room without even telling Laney where you went. I ought to lock you in your damn room and throw away the key."

"Hey, what happened to, 'it's your decision what you do with your body?'"

"I take it back."

"You don't get to take it back. I'm almost eighteen. You won't have custody of me anymore."

"You aren't eighteen yet. Almost doesn't count."

Something occurs to me. "You can't be mad at Cody for this. Don't fire him or make him do a thousand push-ups or anything. I made him go. Laney, too."

"So all of you are fucking Spartacus?"

"Huh?"

"All of you are trying to take the blame."

"Oh."

He closes the door behind him. And locks it. "You might understand more references if you actually watched a movie once in a while. Or TV."

My pulse races. We're alone right now. Very alone. "I prefer music."

A glance at the carved vinyl records. They don't hold his attention very long. His gaze locks on mine. "Since when did I get cast as the Roman general in this little drama?"

I glance at his fists. "Did you hurt a bouncer on your way inside?"

"In my defense, they were standing in my way. I don't take very kindly to people who get between me and my family. Besides, they don't have to be hospitalized. Pretty sure."

My throat feels tight. "Your family."

"That's you, Samantha."

I look away, hiding how much pleasure the word gives me. "Does that mean you'll keep in touch with me when I go on tour? Will you come see me play?"

His expression darkens. "We're not going to be pen pals, if that's what you're asking."

It's a physical blow to my stomach, the dismissal in his words. My instinct is to deny it. He couldn't have meant it. He couldn't have meant it to hurt this much. Then the moment passes and I'm left feeling sick, about to vomit all over the office. "Pen pals?"

Something in his eyes softens. He doesn't look warm exactly, but he doesn't look quite so pissed anymore. "I didn't realize you would want to keep in touch after you left."

The memory of our last talk heats the air between us—about condoms and sex. And the way he walked in on me when I moaned his name. God. I'm not sure I can stand another talk like that. "I'm not naive, Liam. I know you took me in because I didn't have anywhere else to go."

A muscle in his jaw ticks. "That wasn't exactly the reason. And even though I didn't know you before I took custody, I've grown to care about you over the years. If I didn't state it clearly enough, then the fault lies with me. I wasn't raised to show… affection."

I stare at him, incredulous. Affection? It's a cold comfort to a girl who's always wanted the surety of forever. And the word might as well be alien to a man like him. "I'm going to tour the country. The world. I'm leaving, Liam."

He looks away. "Christ."

Unease moves through me. "Did you really think I wouldn't come back?"

"I don't know why you would want to."

"Because I care about you." Liam is six feet of pure muscle and hard will. There's no way someone like me could go up against him and win. Except that when I take a step closer, he tenses. Another step and he goes still as stone. It gives me a sense of power, enough that I take the final step. "I care about you even though you're controlling."

There's only an inch between the ruffle of my blouse and the flat of his abs.

"You think I'm going to apologize for keeping you safe?" he mutters. "You think I give a damn that you're mad at me as long as you're in one piece? That's the only thing that matters."

"Because you think of me like a daughter?"

He shakes his head slowly, not breaking eye contact. "No."

"No?" I whisper.

"When I walked in on you..." His voice is hoarse. "I didn't think of you like a daughter."

I should probably be horrified that he would think about me in any way other than family, except I'm the one who started it. I take a step closer, and there's nowhere for him to go. He's already backed up against the wall. This big, strong man who could probably make a whole army quake—or at least a battalion. And he's cornered by me.

This close I can see the green of his eyes, so dark they're almost emerald, flecked with gold. A scar bisects one dark eyebrow, probably a scar from something terrifying and deadly.

"How did you think of me?" I'm afraid to know the answer, but I'm even more terrified of never knowing. Of being a nameless, faceless body in that writhing crowd, hooking up with a stranger when the man I really want is standing right in front of me, inches away, his breath a feather-touch on my forehead.

A small shake of his head. "It's not right."

I'm not sure what right and wrong mean when it comes to us, but I know what it means for music. Someone can play a piece with perfect timing and notation. They can hit every single note, but it still won't have passion. That part comes from inside. "Then be wrong with me. Don't make me do it alone."

I push up on my toes, pressing my lips against his in a blind, artless kiss. I'm off center of his mouth, kissing the corner. He stands still as a statue, letting me wobble on my heels, letting me fall against him, only my broken kiss to balance me.

Grief beats against my ribs. He's going to make me do it alone. Of course he is. I'm always alone. A small sound escapes me. Loneliness. Pain. It vibrates against his mouth, sound made real.

He jolts as if I've shocked him. Something unspools inside him. I feel it in the inch of air between us. And then I feel it in my lips. He takes over the kiss with shocking possession, his hand behind my head, his body turning us so I'm against the wall. He looms in front of me, blocking out the view. There are no vinyl records on the wall, no bass thrumming through concrete and steel. There's only him, only *this.* How is it possible that only a few minutes ago I felt powerful? I didn't know what this would be. I couldn't know the way I'd revel in surrender.

His tongue touches the seam of my lips, a pure electric sensation that makes me jump. I part my lips in surprise, pulling in the scent of him—man and earth, salt and sea. He tastes elemental. His tongue swipes the tender inside of my bottom lip. It's more sensitive there than I could have imagined. I feel the slickness of the caress all the way in my core. My thighs clench together.

So careful. So wary. I touch my tongue against his. He's the one who groans.

His hand fists in my hair, creating a delicious little ache. "Do you know what you're doing to me?" he breathes, and I try to shake my head; it only makes him pull harder.

"Liam… I need…" It's like the bedroom when he walked in on me, my hips rocking, mindless, hungry. Worse than that. My whole body is moving restlessly against him.

He tears himself away with a hard sound. Only an inch away. A rough tremor runs through him. It's a small comfort, knowing that I've moved this man. Knowing how much control he has, knowing it's eroded. But only a small comfort. He still leaves me panting against the door.

"I'm supposed to protect you," he says, his voice taut with guilt.

"Against people like that?"

"Yes, against people like that. He's more than a club owner, Samantha. At least that's not all he is. He's a loan shark. The dangerous kind. One who makes sure his debts are paid with money or with blood. He doesn't give a shit about doing the right thing."

A shiver runs through me. "How do you know him?"

"I run a security firm. It's my job to know these things." He cups my jaw. "Even if it wasn't, I would make sure to know every single danger within a hundred-mile radius. You're too important to risk."

Determination hardens my tone. "You tell me you want me to make my own decisions as a woman, and then you take them away."

He pulls back, and cool air rushes into the space between us. "Because you lied to me, Samantha. Something could have happened to you, and there'd be no one to protect you, no one to even know where you went. That's not a grown-up decision."

I look down where he's holding my hips in place. It's like prying metal, watching him lift his fingers one by one. Each loss feels like a chain link snapped.

He pulls his hands away with an audible groan. "I'm not going to touch you again."

Hurt licks against my skin like flames, but I try to act casual. "Right."

"If you want to go out, of course you can. I'll send Josh with you."

"Is that an order?"

"Absolutely," he says with burning green eyes.

Despite the hunger in his voice, there's no trace of vulnerability in his expression. He's made of stone and water, as unconcerned as air. Gone is the man incandescent with desire. How am I supposed to be interested in the boys who are dancing in clubs when this man has kissed me? How can I be satisfied with warmth when I know how it feels to burn?

CHAPTER THIRTEEN

Violinist Lindsey Stirling has over 10.5 million subscribers on YouTube.

SAMANTHA

A MESSAGE BLINKS on my phone when I get home from school.

The picture shows a mane of wild red curls, the kind I would have happily traded for my ordinary brown hair. I met Beatrix Cartwright many years ago, back when we were both children.

Our upbringings couldn't have been more different.

She came from a wealthy family, her mother a famous pianist, her father a tech industrialist who doted on his family. Meanwhile my father had to be reminded that my Sergio Peresson violin was on loan from a music society, and we couldn't sell it because they knew who had it. That didn't stop him from threatening to whenever he was particularly broke.

Her parents invested in her musical education and were supremely interested in her feelings. My father only agreed to let me play in the London concert because the queen herself would be in attendance. He spent most of the concert on the phone in the lobby, coming up for air only to glad hand during the reception.

On the surface it seemed like we had very little in common, but Beatrix and I had something in common—we were both children with unusual talent in a world ruled by fierce, egotistical adults.

Somewhere between practice and performance we became fast friends.

Maybe it was fate, which knew we were both on the same dark path. The death of her parents changed the course of her life. I gave her what support I could over e-mail as I followed my father from desert to jungle to tundra, only to begin all over again.

And then my father died, giving us one more thing in common.

Orphans, both of us.

I'm excited about the tour, her text says with a string of green-faced emojis, each of them about to throw up. She's always had a dry sense of humor and a weak stomach.

You're going to be amazing, I text back.

Her anxiety goes beyond stage fright. For many years after her parents' deaths she didn't even leave the penthouse in the hotel where she lived. Only recently did she begin to venture out, but it's still difficult for her to deal with crowds.

I only agreed to it because you're coming, she says. *When do you get here, anyway? Can it be now?*

Words appear on the screen even though I don't feel myself typing them—I'm afraid to leave. I don't want to. What if I never see Liam again? What if he never forgives me for lying to him? The thoughts are too private to be read, even by me.

I hold down the Backspace button until they're gone.

Soon. I punctuate the word with a string of sobbing emojis. Three months, to be exact. It's the closest I can come to revealing my true feelings, the same way the green-faced emojis revealed hers.

How is Liam doing?

Oh you know. The same. Stoic and strong and serious.

So he's being an asshole?

No, of course not. I blush, trying to think of how to word this, how to describe what happened in the back office of the club. I'm not even sure I know the words. Not kiss or touch. Something more meaningful—and more fleeting. *Actually, something happened.*

Uh oh.

It's hard to explain. We sort of... we almost kissed.

Oh my God. Samantha. SAMANTHA. Did he take advantage of you? I'm going to fly to Kingston right now and punch him in the face.

What? Don't be silly, I say, typing quickly because she might actually do it despite her extreme fear of public transportation and the baby girl she has at home. She's only doing the opening show in Tanglewood, which is where she lives. I wouldn't be surprised if the label planted the opening show there just for her.

Beatrix Cartwright is maybe the most famous musician on the tour, besides Harry March himself. She has a massive internet following from playing covers of popular songs and posting the videos online. It's a different direction than the old-world classical music that consumes me, but I admire her skill—as well as her poise in the face of notoriety.

He didn't take advantage of anything, I tell her. *If anything I took advantage of him.*

I'm giving you such a look right now. A look of disbelief.

Really. I'm the one who wants him to see me as more than a child.

But you ARE a child.

I make a rude gesture using an emoticon in response. She's only a few years older than me, and she's already married with a baby. It's actually common for people in our position—strange and rare though it is. We grow up fast and either settle down or burn out.

Well, she says. *I'm sure he turned you down. Liam North doesn't know how to have fun, which has never seemed like more of a virtue than right now.*

Fun? The idea makes me smile. He knows how to fight and work and struggle. The idea of fun is as foreign to him as it is to me. We're well suited that way. *Yes,* I admit. *He turned me down.*

What aren't you telling me?

That makes me sigh. *He really did turn me down. After he kissed me. It wasn't almost anything. We did actually kiss.*

OMG.

Don't freak out. I know it's probably inappropriate.

Probably???

God, how to explain the exhilaration of knowing he had chased after me, bursting into a nightclub, breaking through muscled bouncers to make sure that I was safe. And then the way his large hand had cupped my jaw, making me feel delicate.

I want him to do it again. The cursor blinks at the end of the sentence, waiting with an accusatory rhythm. When I press the Send button, I feel only a sense of rightness. It's honest, at least.

A long time passes with the three little dots hovering where her response will go. She's writing a long lecture about all the ways it's wrong for me to lust after Liam, I'm guessing.

But her text is very short. *What happens when you leave?*

I know what she means. Both of us know what it is to be alone. To be left behind. It doesn't matter that I'm the one walking away this time. Being adrift at sea is no better than being stranded on an island.

Then it's over, I say, knowing there won't be any civic responsibility after that.

LIAM

LEANING BACK IN my office chair, I close my eyes.

The strains of the violin wash over me, soothing the rough edges inside me. I'm in agony thinking of the day when the room next door will be silent. What will happen to every jagged, violent thought inside me?

And even still I look forward to the day that she's gone. Because she shouldn't be near me, shouldn't have to soothe the devil that pants and snorts inside me. A goddamn bull, that's what I am—and her innocence is the red I run toward.

Well, I won't be able to ignore her today. We need to talk about the e-mail from Kimberly Cox. *Good news*, the subject line says. She goes on to explain that Samantha was given a short mention in the digital edition today to raise publicity for the tour, in advance of her deeper profile in the print magazine.

There are a hundred amazing things about Samantha Brooks. The mention could have shared any number of those things. The way she plays like a goddamn angel. The way she mastered violin beyond what most grown men can do at the tender age of six. The way she infuses new life into the classics, drawing the interest of maestros and luthiers from around the world.

Of course the mention doesn't say any of that.

That would make too much sense.

Instead it laments the mark of grief that Samantha still bears from losing her father at a young age. *She used to hide under the desk in his office in Saint Petersburg.*

In fact she was there the fateful day that he died.

The sentence makes my blood run cold. I never should have let the damned reporter speak to Samantha alone. Except that she'll be alone on the tour. I can't stand next to her for the rest of her life, putting limits on how much she says.

I stand and follow the music like she's the goddamn pied piper. I want to follow her anywhere, everywhere, want to drown if that's where she leads me—and I suppose I'm halfway there.

It's my habit to wait until she finishes a piece. The last note sails through the air, sweet and melancholy. There are only four fucking strings on the instrument. She imbues each and every touch of the bow with some new emotion. It reaches into the hard core of me, deadly, devastating.

"Did you read it?" I ask, my voice a harsh echo in the chamber.

She blinks at me as if coming out of a deep sleep. That's what music is for her, a kind of trance. Her cheeks are flushed with awareness.

"Read what?"

"The e-mail from Kimberly Cox, the reporter from *Classical Notes*."

"Oh, about the digital feature? Yeah, that's cool."

Cool. Not the word I would have used to describe it, but then I know that her father didn't die of a heart attack. "They printed the story about your father."

"Right. Well. It would have been more interesting if it were about music, but I guess they figure it was more of a public interest story that way."

"She had no right to share that."

Samantha gives me a strange look. "Are you worried that I'll remember it?"

Yes, but not because of the fear and anxiety the moment would give her. I'm worried that she'll remember it because then she'll know I was there that day. A blessing. That's what the psychologist said about her memory loss. And I couldn't disagree.

I crouch down in front of her, the same way I did when she was twelve years old. Even then she would clutch her violin for comfort. She does it now without even realizing. "Samantha, I told you that your father had enemies. If they think you know something—"

"I was just a child."

Children can be dangerous. This one had always terrified me. "A child who might remember something from when she was hiding under her father's desk. Not only from the day he died. From before that. A phone call. A conversation."

She stares at me, bewildered. "What could I have heard that's dangerous?"

Because her father was a diplomat between politicians who aren't in power anymore. That's what she means. But what she doesn't know is that he was a traitor to his country. That his actions disrupted governments—*this* country's government—with repercussions that continued past his death.

Yes, people would kill to keep those kinds of secrets quiet.

"I'm going to ask you to do something, Samantha. When you do the press for the tour, when the reporters ask you about this, say you don't remember anything."

She blinks. "They're only going to ask about the music."

"Kimberly Cox didn't only ask about the music."

Her brown eyes turn dark. "Are you sorry she

came here?"

She isn't asking about the damn questions. She wants to know about the kiss. I should say yes. I should be sorry that the woman kissed me, that I kissed her back for even a split second, wanting her to be someone else. But that led to me walking in on Samantha. As wrong as it was, it was the single most erotic experience of my life. It was more than I dreamed I'd ever have of her.

To my shame I've jerked off to the image of her in my head every single night. Every morning. My cock throbs in my slacks right now, eager to push through the fabric. To shove aside her skirt and press itself into her warm, welcoming body. She'd let me. She'd beg me to keep going.

"No," I say, my voice rough. "I'm not sorry."

Hurt flashes through her eyes, but I can't begin to explain the complexity of my feelings for her. The way I shouldn't want her. The way I want her anyway. My father always said I had the devil inside me. Part of me never really believed him—at least until I saw her masturbating. It took every last, torn shred of decency I have left inside me to walk away.

Her chin rises, because she's always been so damn strong. She's always deserved better than me. "I'll agree to your rule if you answer one question. Honestly."

My insides tighten. I don't want this bargain, but her safety is worth it. It's worth anything. "What's the question?"

I expect her to ask something about her father, to finally back me into a corner and demand the truth. She deserves that much. *Why did you get custody of me? What happened to my father?* I would have to tell her.

"Did you ever want me?" she asks. "Really want me."

I swallow hard. "That's what you want to know?"

The milestones are coming at me fast, and they're coming hard. Soon she'll graduate from high school. She'll turn eighteen. Those milestones are taking her away from me, bit by bit. None of them compare to what happens when her tour begins. Then she moves to Tanglewood for two months of practice for the tour and the opening show. She'll travel the whole world.

"Yes, I want you," I say, my voice hard. "No, that doesn't even begin to describe… I need you. I crave you. I dream about that kiss in the club."

"Then why won't you—"

"Because you're not eighteen, for one thing. Almost doesn't count."

"What about when I turn eighteen? Isn't there a chance that you and I—"

I would fall to my knees if I thought she should. "I don't see why you'd want to," I say, keeping my voice bland. "You'll have a career then, a record deal, a string of performances under your belt. There will be any number of men."

She reaches out, her hand cupping my face. God, she's innocent. She can't know what she does to my body, the soft touch of her palm, the warmth of her. Or maybe she does know. Maybe she enjoys torturing me. "At the club you said you don't think of me like a daughter."

Slowly I shake my head, my gaze locked on hers. "I don't."

"Then how do you think of me?"

My greatest pride and my deepest regret. And I wouldn't be able to live with myself if I kept her tied here in the middle of nowhere. If I trapped her in the closet with me while I watched her slowly starve. "You saved me," I say simply, unable to lie about this.

Surprise flashes through those pretty brown eyes. "It was the other way around."

"Ah, no, Samantha. I was nothing when you came to me. A man with a death wish. A business that kept me from drinking myself into a stupor every night. When you came to me, it gave me something to live for. Something to believe in."

Enemy fire. Missiles. Ambush. There are things I could handle on the fly, but only one thing could strike fear into my heart—and that's the hope in her eyes. "Then you love me?"

I squeeze her knee and stand up, removing myself from her gaze. "Samantha. I'm sorry. You deserve a family who loves you, but that's not me. I'm not capable of the emotion."

Her eyes glisten with tears before she looks down. "You're wrong."

"And you have unbearably low standards. I only look like a good father because your own was such a bastard. When you go out into the world, you'll understand. You want to come back after the tour? Fine. I'll leave your room the way it is. What do I need it for, anyway? It will keep its pink walls and its white ruffles. And if you tour the world for a year and a half and still want the emptiness that's waiting here for you, you're welcome to have it."

CHAPTER FOURTEEN

Composer Franz Liszt received so many requests for locks of his hair that he bought a dog and sent fur clippings instead.

SAMANTHA

I GIVE LIAM the silent treatment the rest of the week. It makes me feel like a child, but I can't help it. He has all the power in this relationship. All the secrets. Beatrix wasn't completely wrong. He's really a bastard sometimes.

He's also the closest thing I have to family.

It wasn't only him. All three of the North brothers took me in.

Josh taught me how to throw knives even though Liam nearly killed him for it. I'm weirdly good at them. Turns out the upper body strength and nimble fingers you cultivate playing violin translates well to six inches of stainless steel.

I can hit the painted targets almost as well as a soldier.

It was the youngest North brother who drove to the convenience store to buy maxi pads because

I started bleeding when Liam was on an overnight trip. It was my first period. Even if Daddy had been alive, I don't know how he would have handled that. Probably one of his aides would have taught me. Instead Elijah knocked at the bathroom door, grim-faced as he answered my questions—how long would it last and why did it happen.

Probably I should be grateful to have them. So grateful that I don't ask any more questions, but I can't let go of my past. I can't forget the guarded look in Liam's eyes when I asked him about my father. What's he hiding?

It's easy to keep up the silent treatment, because everyone's busy with the wedding. Rows of white chairs replace tractor tires. Flowers overflow rustic wood containers. The entire lawn transforms from a high-impact obstacle course to a romantic lawn in a matter of days. These are soldiers. They perform their mission with precision and fearlessness, even if it involves canapes instead of sniper rifles.

Of course, there probably *are* sniper rifles hidden around the property. I've played the violin in the room beside Liam's office every day for the past six years. I can hear him even when he thinks I'm focused on the strings. He would see the wedding as an opening, something that an enemy could exploit. There would be even more defenses in place today.

Liam is the best man, looking austere and remote in his tuxedo, standing with Hassan at the makeshift altar. There are faint shadows under his green eyes, the only hint that he did anything other than sleep. They're interesting, those shadows, because of how rare they are.

This is a man who doesn't show signs of weakness.

It might be daunting to some brides, the preponderance of stern, muscled men filling the white folding chairs. Jane teaches kindergarten at the local elementary school. Nothing scares her. That's what she told me the first time we met, and it looks like it's true. She's beaming in her white dress with lace that cups her bodice and flares out to a wide skirt.

Hassan swallows hard as she steps out of the tent, his eyes glittering.

Play whatever you want, she told me. *I'm sure it will be beautiful.*

So I play the song I would want if I were to get married, the one I've imagined walking down the aisle to, even though I'd never admit it out loud. Pachelbel composed "Canon in D" to play with three violins and a bass continuo, but I love it even more with a single lilting strain. My Nicolo Amati violin is small and proud. It prefers to play solo. That's where it really sings.

My troubled gaze finds Liam. He's watching me, those green eyes sharp in the sunlight. He owns the land we're standing on, acres and acres of it. He owns the company that employs almost everyone here. He's a leader and a soldier and a confidant to the men beside him.

And he's my guardian. He wouldn't hurt me. I have to believe in that, because without that I don't know what I'd think. I don't know who I could trust.

I try to imbue the words into the bow, into the strings—*I trust you, I trust you.* But I'm afraid they aren't completely true. I love him. I need him, but I don't necessarily trust him. Maybe it's part of growing up to realize that they aren't the same thing—and I'm forced to look away.

He finds me after the ceremony. "We should talk."

I give him a pointed look.

"Still giving me the silent treatment?"

When I was twelve years old, on the cusp of homelessness, of ruin, it was enough to know Liam would take care of me. I didn't need details.

Maybe I didn't want details.

Now it feels scarier not to know, to go into the world misled.

Without a word I tuck my violin case beneath the risers near the house. It's always strange to walk around carrying something worth a quarter of a million dollars. Some people say the violin is like a limb, but it's more than that. It's my heart. My soul.

And it's sitting in a velvet-lined case on the grass. No one would dare steal from Liam North, and technically the instrument belongs to him. How vulnerable it makes me to have something vital to my existence belong to another human being.

A massive white tent covers endless platters of meat, pork belly sliders with homemade coleslaw and beef chuck-eye roast with a paprika herb rub. The bar serves blueberry mojitos with muddled mint leaves and fruit.

A little glass pot contains scoops of warm tri-colored mashed potatoes. I add chives and shredded cheese before carrying it with me, circling the edges of the party. This far away I can see Liam with a mug in his hand, surrounded by people. He's holding court, I realize. Some of the guests are clients of the company. Even wealthy men, successful men, look to him. He grants his audiences rarely with a reserved nod.

He gives approval even more rarely.

Josh slides into the seat beside me, a beer in his hand. "Nice job on the music," he says. "Half the bridesmaids started crying, I have a hell of a time hitting on a girl with mascara running down their cheeks."

That makes me snort. "I wouldn't think that would stop you."

"Well, I'm not saying I'm going to stop."

"If you want my advice, pick one this time." There was an incident last year where he'd lured two women into his bed for a threesome. Except he had only mentioned it to one of the girls. The other one had not been pleased to realize she wasn't the only one joining him.

"In my defense, I was falling down drunk."

"How is that a defense?"

He grins, unrepentant. "She still called me for a date the next day."

I can't help but glance at Liam, where a woman touches his arm as she laughs, leaning close to give him a view down her dress. Will he invite her to his bedroom? There's no question what her answer would be. Morosely I take a bite of the mashed potatoes, but even the buttery carbs can't soothe the jagged edges of jealousy.

"You have nothing to worry about here," Josh says, his voice dry.

"I'm not worried."

"He hasn't slept with a woman in so long I'm pretty sure he's forgotten how. Or maybe key parts of his anatomy have atrophied and fallen off. It's not healthy."

I give him a sideways glance. "How would you know?"

"Because no one who's gotten laid would be that tense."

He *does* look tense. His knuckles are white where he grips the coffee mug. And who drinks coffee at a wedding, anyway? Everyone around him laughs and dances and flirts. These men put their lives on the line every time they take a job. They work hard, and they party even harder. This reception will continue long into the night. It won't stop when Hassan and his pretty new wife leave for Hawaii.

Liam looks like he'd rather be anywhere else.

"Is it the Red Team?" I ask. Those kinds of things are top secret, but you hear bits and pieces when you spend hours outside the office every day.

"Maybe," Josh says. "But I think more than

that, it's the wedding."

"It's beautiful."

"So much happiness and love in the air," Josh says in agreement.

It doesn't take a rocket scientist to figure out that the brothers had a rough childhood. Even this violinist knows that much. Only the details are hazy. "So he doesn't believe in happily ever after?"

"He believes in it for some people. Just not for himself."

The man in question looks this way, as if he can feel my regard. His green eyes burn as he stares at me from across the room. "That's the saddest thing I've ever heard."

"You want my advice?" Josh asks.

"Not really."

"You got a hard-on for your legal guardian? Go for it. You want to work out some good old-fashioned daddy issues with Liam North, be my guest. I'm not the goddamn morality police, and Lord knows he could use the relief. But don't expect anything more from him."

My cheeks flame. Is my lust for his brother that obvious? Even more than embarrassment I'm furious that he would presume to warn me away. "Maybe you're not giving me enough credit.

Someone might be interested in me for more than just sex."

He looks vaguely surprised. "Of course he *wants* you for more than sex. That's not the issue."

Liam must see something on my face, because he starts heading this way. People stop him as he goes, catching his arm. He turns to give them a few words before continuing toward us. "I know I'm not experienced enough for him—"

"He doesn't think he has it in him to love someone."

My heart aches for what could have made him that way. "He's wrong, of course."

"No, sweetheart. That's the problem. He's right."

Liam reaches us in a few long strides, his expression hard. The tan of his skin contrasts sharply with his white shirt. He's removed his tux jacket, which only serves to emphasize the hard, lean line of his body. Silver cuff links glint from his wrists. He's as well-formed as any piece of art, a feast of shape and texture for the eyes—but undoubtedly his eyes are the crown jewels. A deep green like malachite, with darker striations running through them.

Josh stands. "How are you, dear brother?"

The question is asked in a mocking tone, but Liam rarely rises to the bait. Instead he studies me, his green eyes questioning. "Are you all right?"

I press my hands to my cheeks, feeling the warmth raging. *You want to work out some good old-fashioned daddy issues with Liam North, be my guest.* It's hard to find my composure with those words still ringing. "I'm fine," I say on a squeak.

A low laugh from Josh as he wanders away.

"Do I need to kick his ass?" Liam asks, looking grim. It's not an idle threat. In the ways of male siblings, they have been known to throw a punch in an argument. And I have the sense that their past was more violent than most, which may make it worse.

"Absolutely not," I say, keeping my voice light. "He's too hard-headed to learn this lesson anyway."

You got a hard-on for your legal guardian? Go for it.

Somehow I don't think the rest of society would view it in such a light. Things between Liam and me would always be taboo. Always forbidden. It makes me wonder if that makes it sweeter. Then I see the concern in Liam's expression, the wry humor in his eyes, the depth of feeling, and I know I would have wanted him no matter what.

LIAM

THERE'S SOMETHING STRANGE about the way Samantha looks at me. Almost… nervous. Is she afraid of me? Jesus. "Well," I say. "You're probably right. But I'd feel better."

She gives me a droll look that says I'm all talk—which is mostly true. I don't go around beating up people because they say shit to me.

Then again, if they say shit to Samantha, that's a different story.

And her forced casual expression can't quite hide the way her cheeks are pink, her eyes wide as she looks up at me. Definitely nervous about something.

I find Josh outside the tent with one of the bridesmaids, about two seconds away from bringing her to orgasm with the crowd of revelers inside. I clear my throat, which makes him growl his annoyance. "Go away."

He rocks her against his thigh until she comes, biting his shoulder through his tux jacket. Then he whispers something in her ear that makes her giggle, and sends her away on unsteady legs with a pat to her ass.

"God, you're such a bastard," he says without heat.

"You have a bedroom."

"And taking her there would mean giving up on the buffet early."

Naturally he doesn't mean the food buffet. "What did you tell Samantha? She was acting strange after you talked to her."

He rolls his eyes, which is something most men at North Security wouldn't do. That's the thing about working with your brothers. "I told her about the baby bird."

Fury stiffens every muscle inside me. "You did not."

"Oh yes, big brother. Remember that little bird? It had such soft feathers. You wouldn't think feathers could be fluffy, but they were. It had fallen out of its nest."

I have to fight to keep from throwing up on the grass. Wouldn't that be the perfect way to end the day? It's been pure torture watching the happy couple, listening to Samantha play songs about forever and always. And now this.

"Don't," I say, my voice harsh enough that even my brother should know better.

He grins the same way he did as a kid—full of

bravado. He would rather get the shit kicked out of him than admit defeat, and in our house, our father was happy to oblige. "You kept her in your closet, feeding her little bits of bread and peanut butter."

"You did *not* tell this to Samantha."

"So what if I did?" he says, laughing. "She was so sad when I told her about the peanut butter."

I grasp him by the lapels and slam him against a tree beside the tent. "You had no fucking right to do that. You fucking bastard."

He leans his head back, still laughing. "Don't get your panties in a twist. I didn't tell her about the baby bird, or about how Father found out. Or how he locked you in the closet with the bird for days, until you'd practically died of starvation and the bird had died in your hands."

I shove Josh against the tree and push away, breathing hard. "You're a sick fuck."

"Yeah," he says a little sadly. "I come by it honest."

He's still fucked up over what our father did, and I wish I could help him, I really do. All I can do is give him operational command of North Security. All I can give Elijah is the chance to shoot at assholes when they shoot first. That's what our family has come to.

"There's no point talking about the past," I say. "It doesn't matter now."

"Doesn't it?" Josh says, following the path the bridesmaid took toward the entrance to the tent. "Sometimes I think you still haven't let go of that baby bird."

SAMANTHA

I'M THE FIRST one who leaves, slipping into the house with my violin case like a shadow. The faint clatter of dishes comes from the kitchen—the caterers hard at work feeding men who are never really full. I put my violin away with the same care a mother must show her infant child. It might seem extreme to some people, but the violin can't protect itself. It can't wipe away the rosin or polish its wood, so I do it.

In the cool, conditioned air I realize that I've been sweating. The linen of my pale pink dress clings to my skin. Upstairs I take a shower, washing away the scent of the outside, turning my face to the hot spray until I run out of breath.

I slip into my pajamas. Little penguins march across the pale blue flannel. It makes me feel safe and warm—I need that tonight. There are only a couple more months of sleeping in this house.

There's no reason for me to come live here after.

The lights are off when I step into the bedroom. A lamp clicks, and light floods the plush beige carpet. I gasp at the sight of Liam standing near the entrance. His lids are low in the dim lighting, his green eyes burning emerald tonight.

"Going to bed?" he says, the question lazy. Of course I'm going to bed. The question is what he's doing here.

"I'm tired," I say, a little cautious. A little afraid. "Are you going to bed, too?"

He shakes his head. "I thought I'd tuck you in."

Tuck me in? He didn't do that when I was twelve years old. Why would he do it now? The idea wakes up every nerve ending in my body, as if I'm imagining his touch over the blanket, under the blanket, all around me. Nothing about my thoughts is innocent.

He waits while I brush my teeth and change in the closet. I find him sitting on the edge of the bed when I come out, and I climb in, uncertain what comes next.

"Your father made some people angry," he says, his voice low. It's as if the admission is torn from him, and it makes me wonder what else he's been keeping held so tight. He pulls the sheets up high on my body, so it almost touches my chin.

"What does that mean?"

Liam brushes the hair away from my forehead, the touch of his blunt fingertips shocking even in their innocence. "It means he had enemies when he died. Dangerous people who would have hurt you out of a misguided sense of revenge. You couldn't go into the system."

"Is that why you got custody of me?"

"I could protect you."

My throat feels tight. "So you didn't know my father? Not really?"

"I knew *of* him. That was enough for me. The rest doesn't matter."

"Of course it matters," I say, frustrated that he can still pretend this isn't everything. "It's the whole reason you took me in. The reason you turned your life upside down."

"You're safe now, child."

The word *child* makes me rankle with the desire to refute him. But he's sitting on the edge of my twin-size bed, wearing a tux while I'm in jammies. I can't refute anything. He bends to kiss my forehead, and I push him away with a glare. I don't want a chaste kiss on my forehead. I won't accept it.

He frowns. "What exactly did Josh say to you

tonight?"

"He said you believe you can't love anyone. Is that true?"

"I suppose it is," Liam says, sounding unnaturally calm about it. As if it doesn't bother him to miss out on such a thing. "I care for you, though. Is that what you're worried about?"

I sit up in bed. "Tell me something. If you weren't friends with my father, how did you even *know* that his daughter was orphaned? Was there some kind of mass e-mail to people in the intelligence sector? A post in a secret Facebook group? Lost little girl needs a strong and seriously grumpy man to become her guardian."

I'm panting by the time I'm done talking. It's not only myself that I'm fighting for right now—it's him. It's us. And I'm willing to tear down every construct of our guardian-ward relationship to do it.

Unfortunately he doesn't seem to understand the severity of the situation. His lip twitches as if he's holding back a laugh. "Seriously grumpy man?"

"You're like a bear who's been woken up from hibernation."

"Maybe," he allows. "But I have a reason to be concerned about you."

"That's why you freaked out about us going to the club?"

"Well, that and the fact that you're not eighteen yet. Where did you get fake IDs?"

"Look... I have to tell you something about the club." Nighttime is made for confidences, and I have the irrepressible urge to confide in him. Maybe it will become my downfall, trusting Liam. I have to try. "That man—"

"Criminal," Liam corrects gently.

"It wasn't random that I met him there. I went there to find him, so that I could—"

"I know exactly why you went there."

My mouth snaps shut. "Excuse me?"

"You obviously were looking to lose your virginity."

Shock steals my breath, so I can only stare at him in bewildered horror. After a moment I'm suffused with outrage. "And what makes you so sure about that?"

"I understand," he says, with what appears to be sympathy. "You're clearly experiencing a spike in hormones. Maybe even still suffering from some late stage puberty."

I stare at him in undiluted horror. I'm over here thinking about love and sex, about protecting my friend, about a new beginning. And he thinks

I'm having *hormones.*

"Samantha," he says gently.

"No, you're probably right. Hormones. Puberty."

"It's nothing to be embarrassed about."

I'm embarrassed and horrified and most of all, so sad I could cry. Tears prick my eyes. Anger rushes through my veins in a heavy beat. Maybe I actually am experiencing hormones, but that doesn't mean what I feel for him isn't real. "Good night."

CHAPTER FIFTEEN

The violin was considered the leader of the orchestra before conductors became common.

SAMANTHA

IN SOME WAYS Liam North was an indulgent guardian. He would spend two hundred thousand dollars on a violin. He persuaded an infamous violin teacher to move to Kingston so that I could visit him once a week. There were an endless supply of books and music. I always had the latest model phone, some before they were released to the public due to his connections at the major tech companies.

In other ways Liam was the strictest guardian.

My transient existence as a diplomat's daughter had given me its own education. I knew how to barter for fish in an Indonesian market and how to counter the early signs of frostbite, but I couldn't name most of the states. School, he decided. Not private tutors. Not correspondence courses. I should attend an ordinary school with ordinary classes. I'm not sure how ordinary it is to be driven every day by an armed guard in a limo, but St. Agnes did give me a normal experience.

As normal as you can be when the tuition costs thirty thousand a year.

"You ready?" Laney murmurs.

I'm fiddling with the Bunsen burner, nudging the beaker with my tongs. According to Mr. Washington there should be precipitate once the molecules get hot enough to release the sodium. "I'm ready to be done with this experiment."

"Forget about the experiment."

"That's easy for you to say. You're going into finals with a ninety-nine." Laney is freakishly smart, which means she can get straight As without even paying attention. Meanwhile I can't figure out whether I missed something crucial not going to elementary school or whether I'm just naturally terrible at chemistry. If these were sheep intestines that needed to be stretched, if I needed to figure out the precise frequency of a note, I could muster up some interest.

Impatient, Laney taps the beaker. A small pile of white powder appears at the bottom. "We should be grateful he agreed to meet us here."

"Seriously?" I mutter, writing down my findings in the lab notebook. "I know that, but I still don't know how we're going to get past the hall monitors."

St. Agnes could pass for a high-security prison. Every school shooting that happens somewhere in the country is another excuse for them to add metal detectors and cameras—all of it expensive. It makes doing something as simple as skipping class a tactical maneuver worthy of North Security. Luckily I have the daughter of one of the greatest strategists for a partner.

She pulls a key card from her pocket, letting me see it for only a brief moment before slipping it back into her navy blue sweater. "Simple."

I stare at her, incredulous. "You stole Mr. Washington's security pass?"

"Don't freak out. He's always losing his pass, so much that the secretary at the front office keeps an extra one for him in her desk."

"What happens when she sees that it's gone?"

"That won't be for days. We're going to graduate next week."

I'm simultaneously impressed and horrified at how casually my friend has broken the rules. "You realize we're upgrading from breaking school rules to illegal activity, right?"

She scoffs. "What's illegal about swiping a key card?"

"Theft." I tick the words off with my fingers. "Trespassing. Oh, not to mention blackmail."

"All for the greater good."

Acid rises in my throat. If she weren't right about that, I would refuse to do it. I'm not a rule breaker. Not a rebel. At least I didn't use to be. That seems to be changing. "All I'm saying is that if we wind up in jail, I'm blaming you."

"Please. I have about three fake passports that could get me out of the country." At my expression, she adds, "I'm kidding, of course."

I don't think she's kidding. "And leave me here to take the fall?"

Like the way she did at the club. But I know that about her. She's the one who found the guy selling a tape that we can use for blackmail. She also set up the meeting. That's actually a high amount of planning for someone who flew to Coachella in a hot air balloon. I'm the one with the envelope of cash in my backpack. I have to be the one to finish this.

"Nothing is going to happen," she says. "No one is going to fall. This is exactly how my mom got into a Nicaraguan embassy *and* aided the rebellion."

"Which rebellion?"

"Does it matter? We're speaking truth to

power right now. Coach Price is going down."

Because Laney is a smart girl and because it's the only plan we have, I manage to convince myself that everything is going to be fine.

We'll buy the evidence we need to blackmail Coach Price. We'll protect Cody and the other boys he coaches without breaking our vow of silence. And we'll definitely not end up fleeing the country under an assumed name.

At least I believe that until I use the card to get to the tennis court, where the club owner is supposed to be waiting. Only, he's not there. Principal Keller stands there instead.

SAMANTHA

LIAM AND I have sat in the principal's office together before. Once when he enrolled me in the school, after an interview process where Liam drilled the teachers in both core subjects and drama and of course music. Even though it was understood that the serious music learning would happen with my tutors outside school, both Liam and the school agreed that I should participate in orchestra. For the camaraderie, Miss Harper said. If six girls hating my guts for taking first chair every year was camaraderie, then it had definitely worked.

Then again every year as we discussed my progress, my course schedule, my socialization. That's what they called me sitting alone at the lunch table in tenth grade when Laney had volunteered in Costa Rica for a semester.

Daddy never set foot in one of my schools. He would write a note—or have one of his aides write a note. I would take the bus to school, if there was a bus. I also took a train or a rickshaw or in one singular incident in Columbia, a donkey.

And if a teacher ever demanded to see my father, if that was the price of entry, then I simply wouldn't go. *We'll be leaving this hellhole soon enough, Sam.* He called them all hellholes, even if it was a five-star hotel with crystal glasses and gold chandeliers.

Liam showing such an interest in my schooling was strange. Foreign.

And a balm to my grieving little heart.

I repaid him by being the best student St. Agnes had ever seen, forcing my brain to make sense of literature and government when all I really wanted to think about was music.

The number of times he got called to the principal's office for bad behavior?

Zero.

Until today. His expression when he appears at the door is hard. Remote. His green eyes promise punishment. This is the Liam that enemies see when he's in the field, and I shiver in response. I'm the enemy in this situation. I'm sitting in a chair beside the receptionist's desk—probably the same chair where Laney was sitting when she stole that security card.

Thankfully I managed to shut the door in Laney's face before Principal Keller saw her, which means she's in the clear. My fate is yet to be decided.

I make a sound of dismay, of apology.

"Samantha?" he says, his voice severe. I think he wants me to have some easy explanation for what's happening, but I don't even know. How did Keller know I would be there?

"I'm sorry," I say, feeling miserable. I'm not only sorry for him being called in. I'm sorry that I can't confide in him, that as close as we are, we're not close enough for that. Judging from the dark cloud that passes over his expression, he knows what I mean.

Principal Keller appears at the door, a tall man who seems to become more slender every year. His mouth is set in a severe line. "Mr. North. Thank you for taking the time to come today.

Please come in."

Liam looks at me. Apparently he wants me to come in with them. I follow the principal inside with my head down. I take the seat nearest the door, as if I could bolt. Liam sits in the seat beside me, reclined in a pose that's deceptively casual. He shouldn't even fit in the chair. Six-foot-something with lean muscles. The itchy gray fabric on top of a hard-plank of a chair is designed for teenagers. Or maybe adults from fifty years ago. Liam doesn't look bothered by the size of the chair or its questionable stains. Discomfort can't touch him. He looks like he could sit there for years, or that's what it feels like, his gaze heavy on me. My face flames.

Principal Keller clears his throat. "I'm afraid that Ms. Brooks faces serious charges today. We found her with a security pass belonging to a teacher. She used it to leave the building, when she should have been in calculus."

"Is that true?" Liam asks softly.

The principal looks affronted. "I found her outside holding the—"

"I asked her a question," Liam says, without taking his gaze from me. He's going to make me say it. He's going to make me admit the shame out loud.

"Yes," I whisper, not sure whether I'm more humiliated that I did it or that I got caught.

"I'm afraid it gets worse," Principal Keller says, pulling out a familiar white envelope. He sets it on the desk as if it's a proclamation of guilt—and well, I suppose it is. "She had this on her person. A rather large amount of money to be carrying around on a Monday, don't you think? I suppose she wanted to purchase an extra snack at lunch."

Oh great, now he's a comedian. Of course no one laughs. Liam opens the envelope and glances inside, his thumb rifling through the hundred-dollar bills. He's probably counted the money down to the exact amount.

"No doubt she was going to buy drugs," Principal Keller adds.

"Leave," Liam says, his voice low.

My stomach sinks. It's only my worst fear for the past six years, that I would have no place to go, that the one person in the world who cared about me would have enough. Every muscle in my body knots hard enough to make me throw up. I'm clenched on the edge of the hard chair, panic thick in my throat.

Liam looks toward the principal. "We need a minute."

"This is my office, sir." Principal Keller's mouth opens and closes like a fish. "Well, I can see that this is a very serious matter. Probably you want to… one minute, only."

Then we're alone.

I can't relax. He wasn't speaking to me then, but that doesn't mean I'm off the hook. *It was only a matter of time until he got tired of you.* I should be grateful that he kept me around this long. At least I'll have graduated high school, assuming St. Agnes gives me a diploma. I won't have a violin if he kicks me out, but I know how to play.

"Stop that," he mutters.

I swallow hard. "Stop what?"

"Whatever it is you're thinking. It makes me feel like I'm kicking a damn puppy. Don't give me those eyes; you're going to explain yourself. Where did you get this money?"

"It's my violin money." There have been some performances in the space between school—a few concerts over the summer and a trip to Italy last winter break. They pay pretty well. It would have been within Liam's rights to keep the money. After all, he's the one who pays for my school and my clothes. He paid for the violin I used to play.

But he's always kept the money in a bank

account under my name only.

"You were going to spend your violin money on drugs," he says, his voice flat.

"I wasn't going to buy drugs," I say, affronted. Bad enough that he knows I lied to him, that I kept a secret. The thought of disappointing him makes my stomach turn inside out. He doesn't need to think I'm trying to get high on top of that.

"Then what the hell is the money for?"

I press my lips together. Cody and Laney are two of my best friends in the world. I promised them I wouldn't share this secret, but that was before Liam looked at me like I'd disappointed him. "It was for a good cause," I say. "We were going to speak truth to power."

"We?" he asks, his eyebrow rising.

Shit. I'm sure he can guess who my partners in crime are, even if I did manage to keep Laney out of trouble. "Look, the truth is… I can't tell you everything. It's about loyalty and doing the right thing, even when it's hard."

"Christ," he says.

I take a deep breath, tears stinging my eyes. "And if you want me to move out, I'll understand that. I'm almost eighteen, almost graduated high school, and then the tour—"

He makes a slashing motion with his hand. "Move out? You're clearly upset and caught in the middle of something, so I'm going to pretend like that's not a goddamn insult. Did you think that when I took custody of you, it was just for when things were easy? That I would only want you around if you made the goddamn dean's list?"

The way he says it means the answer is no, but I lived too long without any approval to really believe otherwise. My whole life has been about pleasing other people—about making my fingers move fast enough so that someone would clap at the end of the song.

"We're going home," he says, almost growling the words. "Where you will go to your room and think about what you've done. Because you are officially grounded."

CHAPTER SIXTEEN

When violinist Fritz Kreisler served in WWII, his aural sensitivity helped him determine the location of large artillery by listening to the changing pitch of incoming shells across the battlefield.

SAMANTHA

LIAM GETS CALLED away for work on the drive home, which is a relief. It gives me time to rebuild my defenses. Grounded? I've never been grounded in my life. He has no right to do that. And I still don't trust him to do the right thing where Coach Price is concerned.

He might decide to do nothing *and* to block me from helping. That's what he said about the guy at the club, after all. That he would look the other way for local criminals, as long as they left him alone.

That hasn't changed, but we've run out of options. The tapes that we were going to use to blackmail Coach Price disappeared along with the club owner. Liam has the money that I was going to use to buy them, anyway. My violin money—gone.

There's nothing left to do but trust Liam, and the knowledge rises like acid in my throat. I'll have to tell him that Coach Price was doing bad things. That Cody needed us to do this. Maybe he'll consider it his civic responsibility to help. *Like me.*

That night I wander through the halls of the darkened house. Our bedrooms have never been close together, one of the many ways that he's kept distance between us. Ironically I sleep in what's formally the family wing of the house, in the master bedroom. Liam uses a room beside his office to sleep. I have to pass the music room along the way, the shadows heavy, the silence dark. My violin rests in its case, but I feel its uneasy heartbeat as I pass.

A sound comes into the hallway, and I pause on the hard wood.

It was almost an animal sound, grumbling and dangerous. I take another step. Another. There's only quiet now, but the hair on the back of my neck rises.

Then I hear it again—a growl of warning.

Blood races through my veins. I may not fully trust Liam, but he's the only place I feel safe. His door is cracked open, revealing only a blanket of darkness. I push inside to safety, glancing over my shoulder, my pulse a hard staccato in my throat. Closing the door, I lean against it, panting.

Only to realize the sound is coming from inside the room.

A form writhes on the bed, large, menacing. A wild sound of rage. Of pain?

"Liam?" I whisper.

My eyes adjust so slowly, revealing a feral animal, revealing a man in sleep. White sheets are tangled around his waist. His shoulders are thick with muscle. He grasps the sheets, the pillows, fighting something. My heart clenches at the realization.

Liam North is having a nightmare.

I put my hand on his shoulder. Tension ripples beneath my palm. He's facing down, fighting some invisible enemy, sweat a faint gleam across a landscape of strength.

He goes still.

"It's just a dream," I say, soothing. Only it doesn't feel like a dream. There are terrible demons in the room, as living and breathing as I stand here. Maybe more.

A crash of motion, and then I'm pulled, twisted, pinned onto the bed. I land hard on the expanse of cool sheets. Breath leaves me in a rush. A large body cages me from above, an arm pressed across my neck. It's not hard enough to keep me from breathing, but I definitely can't move.

"Liam," I say, gasping. "*Liam!*"

He trembles above me, around me. He's become my whole world—and it's a dark place to live. His breath saws through the air like a serrated blade.

"How dare you," he says, his voice guttural.

He's asleep, he's still asleep, and I don't know how to wake him up. Only then his hand moves from my neck to my jaw.

His thumb brushes over my cheek. "Samantha," he mutters.

"I'm sorry," I say, more for whatever horrors haunted him in the nightmare than for waking him. Someone should be here every night, to pull him back to the land of the living.

"I could have hurt you." He sounds hoarse but coming awake. "Do you have a goddamn death wish, Samantha? I could have killed you."

I'm trembling underneath him, still trying to make sense of how I ended up on his bed, how I ended up between his thighs, the heavy weight of *something* on my stomach. "You wouldn't hurt me," I say, the words coming breathless and unsure.

The smell of him—earth and musk and salt. It's all I can think about, the way he surrounds me. The way he moves over me. This is how it would feel if we made love. Even his arm across my neck... it's meant to be a violent act, but it feels sensual. My nerves pick apart every sensation: the heat of him, the rasp of hair across his forearm, the throb of his pulse.

This is every erotic dream I've ever had, everything I see when I close my eyes, my hands between my legs. It would be perfect—if he wasn't still trembling from aftershocks. What kind of terrible thing would make Liam so scared he would lash out like an animal? He's the most controlled person I've ever met.

He dips his head, his lips against the curve of my ear. "I would," he murmurs, but it sounds like he's trying to convince himself. "You aren't safe with me."

The words resound inside me. I'm not sure they're true, but I'm sure he believes them. Don't they match what I thought when I came here? That I can't trust him. That I would be a fool to trust him... and yet, seeing him in the throes of his nightmare has changed everything. He's two hundred pounds of solid muscle straining above me, but he's the vulnerable one right now.

I run my hand over his back as if I can soothe him.

As if I can tame him.

LIAM

MY MIND REELS from the sudden break of night.

Darkness blankets the bedroom, but not like my dreams. It's not the lack of light that makes dreams dangerous. It's the lack of hope.

Breath saws through my throat. Every muscle is pulled tight, ready to strike. Slowly, slowly, the shadows form into the shape of a person. Samantha looks up at me, her eyes wide with fear.

"Christ," I say, my voice hoarse. "What the fuck are you doing here?"

She blinks at me, her mouth open. That's when I realize that I still have my arm across her neck. She can't breathe. I'm hurting her. I swore I'd never hurt her.

I pull back enough to let her breathe, but something strange happens. I can't stop touching her. I'm clutching her, feeling her, making sure she's not broken or bruised. My hands are rough. I'm probably making it worse, but I need to feel her solid and warm and alive.

A ragged breath. Another. Her slender body shakes underneath me, her eyes watering. "I'm fine," she says even though it's clearly a lie. "Fine."

"Fine," I repeat, grim and sick with it. "You're the furthest fucking thing from fine. I could have killed you, Samantha. Do you understand that? I could have crushed your windpipe in a second."

A shiver takes her body. She's scared of me.

As she should be.

It's not a regular man who got custody of her six years ago. I hide the feral part of me, but it's inside, waiting to get out. "Don't ever do that again—Jesus, don't. Don't cry."

Tears slip from her eyes, but she doesn't make a sound. That hurts almost more than if she'd sobbed in my arms. I learned violence in my childhood. She learned to hide her pain.

"I'm not hurt," she whispers.

"You are," I say, insistent. She's hurt in so many ways she can't even count them all. She came to me shattered. The bastard of a father had neglected her in a thousand ways for the first twelve years of her life. And then he'd died. My fault. It was my fault he was gone, and the worst part is that I'd never once regretted it. Not when it brought her to me.

Her palm cups my face, rubbing gently. Her skin is so soft, impossibly fragile as it rasps against a day's growth on my jaw. "What were you dreaming about?"

My entire body reacts to that—a sudden jerk, as if she slapped me instead of caressed me.

What was I dreaming about? I don't want that near her. Not even the description of it. Not even the thoughts. "It doesn't matter."

Her eyebrows draw together. "Was it from when you were overseas?"

From my time as a soldier. Yes, there were some dark moments. Blood and death. That's probably what I should be having nightmares about. I'll send my brain a fucking memo, because it can't seem to get over what happened years before that. "No."

"You sounded…" She swallows. "Afraid."

Afraid. Yeah, I'd been afraid. It had buried itself deep in my skin, and all these years later, even knowing that no one can hurt me, it hasn't left. The irony is that it made me a beast on the battlefield. I wasn't afraid of a goddamn IED blast. Nothing in that godforsaken desert could scare me. There'd been a time in my life it would have been a blessing.

Another tear rolls down her face, and I realize

she isn't crying because I hurt her. She's crying because I'm hurt. Something strange tightens in my chest. I basically attacked her like an animal, like a fucking animal, and she's worried about me.

"It doesn't matter what I dream about. The important thing is that you never do that again. Why did you come here?" But for some reason I can't make myself let go of her.

She's still underneath me, her body warm and quivering.

My cock is hard. The warmth of her, the sweet scent of her. She must feel my erection where I'm straddling her. Does she know what it means? *Of course she does, you bastard.*

"It does matter," she says, squirming a little in ways that make my cock flex against her flat little stomach. "It matters what you're dreaming about."

My body doesn't feel like it's under my control. I want to blame the nightmare, but this isn't something I ever thought about when I was five years old in a goddamn well. I dip my head to breathe her in. Maybe the scent, one deep breath—it might be enough. It's not. I need more. I press my face against her neck. The bristles on my jaw rasp against her. My lips follow to soothe away the sting. Her breath catches, and

I can't make myself stop.

"I'll prove it to you," I mutter, my voice almost a growl.

Her eyes widen, dark pools that I could drown in, but she doesn't look afraid.

She looks curious.

How can I send her out into the world like this? So damn innocent. So trusting, when she has no idea all the ways I want to use her. I close my fist hard, pulling her hair taut, exposing her neck, a pale column against the wild shadows of her hair.

A squeak escapes her, but that's not enough to make me stop. She'll be alone on that tour, at the mercy of men like Harry March, men who don't have any morals. Men like me.

I press my hips down, rubbing my erection against her small body. She has to know what she's up against. She has to know what I want.

She wriggles underneath me, probably trying to escape. All it does is make me harder. I'm so much bigger than she is, so much stronger.

"Tell me no," I say, my words hard and cold. "Fight me."

"What?" she gasps.

"You have to be safe." It's become a prayer. A promise. "If a man tries to touch you… You have to protect yourself from people like me."

That's the part I didn't say during our sex talk. The part I couldn't bring myself to say. Couldn't bring myself to think about. Samantha, hurt. Samantha, afraid. Until I was twenty thousand feet above the ground, watching her sneak out on the goddamn video camera, ice in my veins.

And still she blinks up at me. There's an entire universe inside her. Creation and destruction. A million stars lighting up the night.

"What happens if I don't say no?" she asks. "What if I say yes?"

Oh God, she's testing me. Tempting me. She has no idea what she's asking for, what I could do to her before she has a chance to object. *Show her*, the devil inside me whispers.

It sounds like my voice, that devil. It's me.

I lean down, my lips an inch from hers. But I don't do anything as sweet or ordinary as kiss her. That would be too much like romance, too much like love, and those impulses were beaten out of me a long time ago. Instead I bite her lip, tugging her tender flesh between my teeth.

It's a threat, the way I give her a little pressure, only enough to hurt. I won't leave bruises, but I want to. That's how fucked up I am. I want to leave my mark on her body, on her soul.

I've never let those impulses out of their god-forsaken cages, but it's happening now. I trail my lips to her jaw and scrape her velvet-soft skin with the edge of my teeth. If this is what it takes for her to understand the threats, for her to protect herself from the dangers out there in the world… if this is what it takes to keep her safe…

That's the excuse I tell myself as I grasp her earlobe between my teeth.

Peaches. Vanilla. Sweetness and cream.

Her scent reaches inside my lungs, imprinting on me the way I want to imprint my will on her. Something feral takes over my body. I'm acting on pure instinct as I burrow closer to her. Down the smooth line of her neck, where it meets her shoulder. That's where I bite her.

She jolts beneath me, making a sound that's every bit as animal, a sound of submission and pleasure. It would be so easy to pull her nightshirt up, to rip her panties to shreds. To push my aching cock inside her little cunt and finally have relief.

"Yes," she whispers as if she can read my thoughts. "Please."

Her small hands grasp my shoulders, my chest, my abs. She rocks herself up, thrusting her flat belly against my erection, and I grunt at the terrible pleasure. God.

Even more than I want to fuck her, I want to eat her. To bite my way down her lithe body, to sink my teeth into her hips, her thighs. To lave my tongue right between her—

"No," I choke out, pushing back from the bed. There's physical pain, removing myself from her clumsy embrace, as if I cut off a limb. My cock throbs in my briefs. It knows how close it came to heaven.

"Tell me what the money was for."

SAMANTHA

I'M PANTING IN the erotic haze he left me in. This is probably some kind of military interrogation technique, to make someone writhe and shudder. And then ask her a question. My brain is too muddled to come up with a lie. And worse than that, my defenses are down.

Slowly I sit up on the bed and grab a pillow to clutch in my lap, but it's not much of a wall. It doesn't protect me from his harsh breathing or the broad silhouette from the moon in the window.

"Okay," I say, my voice trembling only slightly. "I'll tell you."

There may as well be a marble statue in the room with me for how still he is, except that he's emanating heat at approximately ten thousand degrees. It radiates from him in furious demand.

"There's a new coach at Kingston High." There are really only two high schools in the city, the public high school with its large football stadium and massive prom nights. And St. Agnes, which is where Laney and I attend. "Cody told us that he's… that he's watching them. Touching them."

My cheeks flame at the words.

A low growl fills the room, raising the hair on the back of my neck. "Touching them?"

"Not like that," I say quickly. "At least not yet." I heard this only secondhand. Cody confided in Laney, who broke his confidence enough to share it with me.

"Then what is it like?" Liam bites off the words.

"He gives them a hug if they lose a game. Or he'll give a player a massage if he has a tight muscle. Things like that." I shake my head, struggling to explain. We couldn't go to the authorities with something like that, couldn't risk everything on a bad feeling. What if no one believed us? What if Coach Price retaliated against

Cody for saying something? The boys already started pairing off when they go to the locker room, but it's only a matter of time.

"What was the money for?" Liam asks, his voice strangely calm. Gone is the panting, raging man who hovered over me only a few minutes ago. This is the high-paid security operative. "Were you trying to pay him to leave?"

"Kind of. It was for a video."

"A video of what?"

"I don't know," I confess, my cheeks burning in the dark. "Laney did some digging at the school in Austin where he worked last. Apparently there was some scandal that they hushed up. And this guy had some kind of incriminating video file."

"So you were going to buy the video. And then what?"

I blink. "What do you mean?"

His voice goes subzero. "What were you going to do with the file, Samantha?"

That was the easy part, wasn't it? Only we never got that far. "We'd blackmail him, make him leave the boys alone, make him resign his position."

A low growl. "Did it occur to you that he might have bought your silence a different way? By hurting you? Threatening you? Killing you?"

My stomach turns over. "We would have been careful."

The long pause that follows makes me think of every bad thing that could have happened to Laney or Cody. If anything would happen to me, I know that Liam North would blame himself.

"Careful," he says, his voice hollow. "There is no amount of careful that would be good enough. How dare you risk your life like that? Do you know what I would do if you—"

Shock makes me breathless. "You risk your life all the time. You send men and women to risk their lives for North Security. But I can't do the same thing?"

"No, goddamn you."

I flinch from the venom in his voice. "That's not fair."

"Life isn't fair, Samantha. That's something Cody and his teammates already learned, and it's something you're going to have to learn, too."

"So you aren't going to do anything to help?"

"It's not my business."

Acid rises in my throat. "What if you had said that about me?"

Something dark moves through the forest of his eyes. "I didn't."

"What's so different between me and Cody?

Why would you help me but not him?"

"Don't ask me that, Samantha."

"No! I've had enough of being quiet, of being the good little girl who does what she's told. If you won't help him, I'm going to."

A harsh laugh. "Don't push me. I'm about two seconds away from locking you up."

Indignation and a strange secret desire rise inside me. The indignation wins. "You can't lock me up. I'm an adult now."

"Almost an adult. And as I said before, almost doesn't count."

He makes me so angry, there may as well be steam rising from my ears. I clutch the pillow tighter, wondering about whether I should throw it at him. But then I would lose my shield.

I don't know why a twelve-year-old girl he'd never met mattered to him when a boy who lives in the same city doesn't, but I'm not above using that to my advantage. "What if I ask you to?"

He freezes. "Ask me to what?"

I stand up from the bed and take a step closer to him—and almost, almost touch him. "You can use my violin money. If you buy the video, he won't be able to hurt you."

"You want this from me?"

A solemn nod.

The closet light flicks on, blinding me. His body blocks it, and then he's getting dressed right in front of me. Worn jeans pulled on over his briefs. A T-shirt covering his abs. I've never watched him get dressed before, but there's something studiously casual about his movements.

As if he's hiding a black hole of emotion.

I'm wearing a tank top and panties, the same as I do every night. The same as I was when I walked in here, but I feel more exposed now that he's wearing regular clothes.

The closet light casts his face in sharp contrast, the stark handsomeness of his features abutted against pure dark. "I'm not going to give that man a single goddamn cent, but if I did, it sure as hell wouldn't be your violin money."

There's a boulder in my chest, crashing left and right. "You're going to do it?"

"I'm going to do it," he says, his tone grim, and I can't shake the feeling that something powerful is in play, more than a guardian doing a favor for his ward.

"Tomorrow?" I ask.

He gives a low growl of assent. "Tomorrow."

"You're not… mad. Are you? About what happened?" I can't quite look back at the bed where we were. I have only the fleeting impression of rumpled sheets. Sheets that had held Liam's muscled body.

"At you? No."

Acid rises in my throat. Oh, he's going to blame himself. "Liam."

He ties a knot with hard, efficient movements and stands. "You'll stay here where it's safe until I have the video. I'll have Josh watch you. No sneaking out again."

Such a parental thing to say. "You didn't do anything wrong," I tell him, earnest, desperate to save what I've already lost. I can feel the grains of sand between my fingers. "You didn't hurt me. You only—"

You only bit me.

A humorless laugh is my answer. "The coach is abusing his power. You were the one telling me how wrong it is, how I should stop him. How is what I did on that bed any different?"

"Because I wanted it."

He shakes his head, turning away from me. "That doesn't matter."

His broad back will be the last thing I see of him, on the one night he sees me as more than a child. I can't let him leave this way. I'm done letting him tell me what to do. "It matters."

I'm standing in his bedroom, my bare feet

rooted to the ground. He's in the doorway, his whole body tense as if he needs to flee. Well, maybe he does. Maybe he can't handle what he wants or what I want. Maybe he can't handle me, but I'll be damned if I let him think he's doing this for my own good.

"What did you say?" he asks, his voice soft.

Anyone else would be wary to hear that tone. Anyone else would be terrified, but he had his chance to hurt me. He could have done so on the bed. And he could have hurt me worse, so much worse, if he hadn't agreed to help me with Coach Price.

My voice still quavers as I stand my ground. "Rebels took the embassy in Jakarta. I was five years old, and I hid in the cabinets until they found me the next day."

He makes a low sound of protest. "What's your point?"

"The motorcade left me behind outside Moscow. It took my father two days to realize I wasn't there. I hiked to the nearest village and begged them to let me stay in broken Russian."

"So your father was a bastard," he says, his voice flat. "I already knew that."

"I grew up faster than anyone at St. Agnes, and you know it. I may not be experienced with… sex things, but I know what I want. And that's you."

He looks so alone standing there, a fortress that will never be torn down, self-contained and isolated. I let myself think that he might let me in, that he might trust me the way I'd brought myself to trust him. It's enough to make my breath quicken, this hope. This longing.

When he turns away from me, it shouldn't be a surprise. The weight of it shouldn't crush me. I've had a brick wall around me since I was a child.

Only Liam has the power to tear it down.

"Let me stay," I say softly.

"Why?" he asks, his broad back still and dark like a statue in the room.

"Because I have nightmares, too."

He'll leave now. That's the only thing he can do. The only thing he'll allow himself to do. I'm not the only one with a brick wall around me. He has his own, and I've never been able to breach it. Which is why I'm not expecting it when he pulls me into his arms. He carries me to bed, holding me tight through my tremors of shock and years-long relief.

That's how I fall asleep—with him protecting me in the most elemental way, blocking out the bad thoughts with his body. I use him as a shield, but I do more than that. I shield him, too. When he's holding me, the darkness can't reach us.

CHAPTER SEVENTEEN

Violin strings were originally made from dried sheep intestines.

LIAM

IN THE DAYS that follow, I pay a visit to the club where I found Samantha and get the tape—using my reputation and intimidation rather than her precious violin money. I meet with local police and school board members. Coach Price is stripped of his position with the kind of expediency that can only come from a massive scandal. Or in this case the threat of one. A generous endowment to the school's sports program means they'll be able to hire a new coach and renovate the gymnasium.

I may have resisted this errand at first, but I find it gives me a sense of satisfaction to make this right, to do something for Samantha.

And in the nights that follow I'm confronted with the worst kind of temptation. I go to sleep alone, certain that I can smell Samantha, that I can feel her body heat left over.

She tiptoes into my room around midnight. I wake up wrapped around her small body, her soft hair in my hands, my nose pressed to her skin, my dick aching from being hard for hours with no relief. It's an exquisite torture, wrong on every level, and I never want it to end.

On the fifth night I wake to find her legs wrapped around me, our bodies aligned in the most carnal way, my dick throbbing against the heat it can feel through the fabric of my briefs and her panties. Bad enough that I gave in and kissed her in that club. I'm not going to thrust against her until she comes. I'm not, I'm not. I repeat the words until they become a chant, a plea to a God I never believed in.

Carefully I pull her limbs away from me, untangling our bodies, until she clasps a pillow close and settles back into sleep. Then I cross the large bedroom to the bathroom and close the door. *Christ.*

Thinking of tactical formations isn't going to help. The only thing that will bring down this erection is to jack off. I turn on the shower and set it to scalding hot.

Steam coats the glass.

I step inside and grasp my dick, which aches like a motherfucker. It doesn't want the calluses on my palm or the rough, angry tugs. It wants to be encased in soft, wet velvet.

My eyes fall shut, and I imagine that she's in the shower with me, her skin slippery, droplets running down her breasts. I would catch them as I suck on her nipples. I would drink the warm water in open mouthed kisses along the flat of her stomach. It would taste like nothing, nothing at all, until I'd slide my tongue between her legs, finding salt and desire.

Water trails down my body, and I imagine that it's her tongue, finding the dips and rises of my muscles. She would get on her knees in front of me and lick her pink lips.

A little sound makes my eyes fly open.

Samantha stands in the doorway to the bedroom, her mouth parted in surprise, her eyes wide in unmistakable arousal. There's enough steam coating the glass to make her hazy, as if she isn't quite real, the sweetest dream I've ever had. I should stop, I should absolutely stop touching myself, stop fucking myself. Instead I squeeze hard from the base to the tip, punishing myself for how good it feels.

At the very least I expect her to flee the room, but she stands there, watching me with hunger in her dark gaze, with an innocent curiosity that makes my blood run hot.

And then she takes a step closer.

I plant my hand on the cool tile and use the other one to pump my dick. And then I still my fist, moving my hips instead, thrusting the way I want to do inside her body. I would hold her head as the water came down around us, using her sweet mouth until I came in a blinding rush. My cum would fill her mouth, and she would have no choice but to swallow it down. I'd catch clear water on my fingertips and feed it to her to wash me down. Then I'd reach down between her legs, make her climax as she knelt on the smooth tile of the shower, legs splayed and useless, arms clinging to my leg in surrender, the salt of my sex still on her tongue.

Every thought is in my eyes as I watch her, and she seems to know it—if not the exact contents, at least the spirit of it. She takes another step closer, and then another, until the only thing between us is the steamed glass of the shower door.

She puts her hand on it, her palm toward me, fingers spread.

I touch her hand through the glass, as if I can feel her.

My forehead rests on the glass, needing the

connection, every part of me straining to break through the tempered glass and touch her, how soft she would be, how warm, as I come with a shout of forbidden pleasure, my whole body convulsing, hips fucking the air, my cock in agony as it comes in the warm, humid air instead of her tight cunt.

My head bows as I catch my breath, panting like an animal in the aftermath.

When I look up again, she's gone. The doorway is dark. I can almost believe that she was part of my fantasy, not a real person who watched me come, except for the small handprint breaking up the steam on the other side of the glass.

God, she's probably run back to her room—and no wonder. I should never have kept touching myself when she walked in. Then again this is my bathroom. My shower. The lines between right and wrong have blurred so much that I don't know where to begin.

The only thing I know for sure is that I want to fuck her so bad it hurts.

Dressing quickly, pulling on a T-shirt and briefs over my wet skin, I head into the bedroom. I'll have to find her in the house and make sure I haven't scared her. Except she's lying in bed where I left her, her dark eyes catching light from the bathroom and throwing it back to me in the dark.

"Are you okay?" I ask, my voice low.

"Yes," she says. "Why wouldn't I be okay?"

So she doesn't want to talk about it. I should tell her to go back to her room. It isn't appropriate for her to be here. Except that she wasn't lying about having nightmares. Sometimes she cries out in her sleep. Remembering the night her father died?

Part of me wants to rage at her for leaving. Part of me wants to push her out of the fucking nest, to let her fly or fall, not to catch her on the way down. It isn't in me to make her leave, so I climb back into bed with her. She curls herself against me, her hair dampened from standing in the bathroom, steam rising from both of our bodies.

LIAM

I'M ASLEEP WHEN the call arrives, but my body is trained to come fully awake at the first sign of trouble. I suppose I would have cultivated that skill in the military if I needed to.

I had it the day I enlisted. That's what comes of growing up with a man who believed the devil resided in you. My childhood was a study in wild opposites, the intense high of an exuberant, loving father, and then the inevitable turn that came at night. He would charge into my room because of some nightmare he had, a sense that the devil was inside me, determined to drive him away. Anything that had happened during the day, a phrase I had used or an expression on my face, could be caused by the devil. My father would do anything to drive him out—press my hands onto the lit burner of the stove, choke me until I passed out. Throw me into the well so the cold and damp would drive away evil spirits.

The red light blinks on my phone, which means it's coming in from a secure line. We have servers set up so that teams on deployment can reach us from anywhere without our location, and thus their identity, being compromised. "Hello," I say, my voice hoarse as if I've been shouting in my sleep. I didn't even realize I still had nightmares about the well until Samantha woke me up. She's sleeping soundly in bed right now, and I take a few steps away, toward the bathroom, so I don't wake her up.

A female voice identifies herself using a nine-digit alphanumeric code, her latitude and longitude, and an abbreviation that means she's not being coerced to make this call. Laney's mother. That's a fucking relief. The last thing we need is another orphan around here.

"Sitrep," I say, already pulling on my jeans. I give Samantha a last glance before I shut the door to my bedroom, keeping her shielded from the darkness in my world. This is one area where I won't compromise her safety.

"We ran into some trouble during our exfil from the region. A local drug lord and pimp was making an example of one of his girls. The team commander took exception."

Striding through the hallway, I almost collide with Josh, who's heading to the office. He got the same notification that I did about the secure line and probably hit the Answer button a millisecond after I did, barely missing the call. He managed to pull on a shirt, which is one step more than I did. His eyes are alert, but he doesn't say anything, waiting for me to finish the call.

"Where is the team commander?" I ask, flipping on the lights.

"Uncertain. He ordered us to hang back while he scoped out the situation."

I press two fingers to my brow where a sharp pain slices my skull. There's a wealth of problems in a handful of words. As the team commander, Elijah's word would be final on a situation. Team members like Laney's mother could advise him, but he had the final say—chain of command is crucial to these missions. Of course, sticking to the objective is also crucial.

An objective that has nothing to do with a local drug lord.

"What were his exact orders?"

"He told us to go dark until we met up at the rendezvous point, which would have been this morning. We waited three hours past the mark before retreating."

"Are any of you injured?"

"Negative."

Christ. I give the sitrep to Josh, who swears in a long and creative streak.

"He wasn't going to *scope out* the situation," Josh says, biting off the words. "He was going to assassinate the fucker, and probably start an international incident while he's at it."

Unfortunately there's a very real possibility of that. While no one would cry over a shitty drug lord, the balance of power in these places is precarious. It's even possible this person was backed by the local authorities, making Elijah the target of a corrupt government. "At the very least it sounds like he may have gotten himself captured."

"Or killed," Josh says. "And endangered his team in the process."

Any other employee of North Security would have found himself fired for even a fraction of the breaks in protocol. Elijah North is more than an employee. He's our brother. Which means I'm more interested in finding his ass than firing it—and then giving him a well-deserved black eye.

"Hold your position," I say into the phone. "We're sending reinforcements."

It will take at least twelve hours to get on the ground there, but I'm not going to send the team looking for them when they're already a man down and probably half-frozen from hiding out in the godforsaken wasteland that is northern Russia. I give her details of a rendezvous point for us to meet while Josh notifies the pilot to get his ass out of bed.

"Three men," I say when we're both off the phone. "I don't want to send in the whole Blue Team now that I know the situation. Who knows what kind of fucking drug turf war we're walking into. Quiet as a fucking mouse. Lewis and Jameson."

"And you?" Josh says, raising his eyebrows.

It's hardly uncommon for me to join a mission, especially one as crucial as this one. If word gets out that North Security was in the area, fucking around with criminal activity, then it means our true objective will also be exposed. "Do you have an objection?"

A sardonic rise of his brow. "Samantha's graduation."

How could I forget? There are a thousand dates in my head, but I don't want to think about her graduation. It's one step closer to taking her away from me.

Her graduation and then her birthday. And then the goddamn tour.

We're only a month away from it now. I would give almost anything not to attend the damned ceremony with her self-righteous principal and the piece of paper he'll give her that says she's all grown-up.

I would give anything not to attend, except that it would hurt Samantha. That's pretty much the one thing I'm not willing to do. "You're right," I say, gruff in my sense of loss.

"I'll bring Elijah back," Josh says, sounding grim. And of course he will.

Elijah's the youngest of the three of us. For a time it looked like he would turn out the most normal. He was going to marry his high school sweetheart, until she was kidnapped on her senior trip. It's been years now, but I think some part of him thinks she's still alive somewhere. That poor girl that the pimp made an example of, she could have been the girl he loved.

Hell, I probably would have done the same thing. If Elijah wasn't successful in exterminating the pimp, I'd help him do it. The girl would have reminded me too much of Samantha, at the mercy of terrible men.

Of what could have happened to her if I hadn't gotten custody.

CHAPTER EIGHTEEN

"I love power. But it is as an artist that I love it. I love it as a musician loves his violin, to draw out its sounds and chords and harmonies." – Napoleon Bonaparte

LIAM

"A DAMNED EMBARRASSING business," a man says.

I recognize him from the St. Agnes Board of Directors, of which I'm also a member. It's a fancy name for parents who've paid enough money to ensure their children get special treatment at the elite private school. Or in my case, my ward.

We're standing in a room with three hundred chairs and a makeshift stage while we wait for the students to emerge in their caps and gowns. The room is abuzz with proud parents, with boasts of honors and Ivy League colleges.

"The business about the coach from the public school," he explains. "It's a shame what happens for the regular kids in this country."

"A shame," I echo, keeping my tone bland. "If only there were people in a position to give their time and money to improve them."

He gives me an uncertain look. "It falls to their parents, of course."

"Of course." The working parents of the kids at Kingston High are barely keeping food on the table, much less personally vetting every new hire at the school. And most of them don't have the money or clout to expose a predator like that, even if they suspect something.

No, I'm well aware that it falls to men like us to protect the children in our communities. My shame comes from how long it took me to understand that.

I needed Samantha to convince me.

My phone buzzes. "Excuse me," I tell him, stepping away.

Found him, it says from an undisclosed number.

I type in the reply quickly. *Alive?*

Unfortunately.

Relief fills me. That would be Josh's sense of humor. He wouldn't be making jokes if our brother Elijah were seriously injured.

Josh thinks he's being clever and incisive—and damn him for being right. What he said about the baby bird at the wedding? I'm still thinking about that, when I had almost forgotten. If not forgotten, at least buried deep enough to slowly poison me from the inside. Close enough.

My stomach clenches hard.

On the first day we'd been locked inside, I had run my fingers through the pile on the carpet, into the seams of my pockets, searching for crumbs to feed her.

On the second day I had wrapped the baby bird in an old sweater so it would stay in the corner, safe and unharmed, while I rammed my shoulder into the door again and again, until the wood splintered—but did not break—and my shoulder throbbed.

On the third day I'd simply held her, whispering things about blue skies and a ground full of delicious worms. I told her how soft she was, what a good baby bird, as she grew more and more quiet. Until she finally stilled, falling asleep for the last time.

I have tickets for a box at Samantha's opening show. At the next one and the next one. Maybe it's fucked up that I could have followed her whole goddamn tour, but I realize now that I can't. It would be like trapping her in the closet with me.

She would never survive, and I would have to watch her slowly die.

SAMANTHA

THE GRADUATION CEREMONY at St. Agnes takes twice as long as the one at Kingston High, even though we have a fraction of the number of students. There are speeches by the principal and the counselor. Laney gives a moving speech as the valedictorian, one about loss and the intractability of hope—all the more meaningful because her mother isn't home for this.

The commencement speech comes from a former senator, who speaks to the small room as if we were gathered on the lawn of Princeton.

The senator's pale eyes flicker with recognition when my name is called. Samantha Alistair Brooks. Despite the smattering of fan mail I get every week, I'm not really famous outside the music world. I doubt he read the in-depth article in *Classical Notes*.

He probably knew my father.

Tension knots in my stomach as I climb the short steps.

My gaze crosses the room, past the rows of proud parents in bamboo chairs, to the man in the back. Liam North stands with a sense of resolve, as if facing some dangerous enemy, resolute in the face of death. His eyes have turned dark emerald, unreadable as I cross the stage.

Principal Keller gives me a grim smile and the same murmured praise in Latin that every other student receives. I'm sure he's glad that I'll be gone from the school. Doesn't matter that I graduated in the top one percent. Liam made it clear that I would not perform on behalf of the music department during the interview, which means that despite having a semi-famous student, they could never use me.

At least I didn't get expelled shortly before graduation.

The senator also greets every student, a practiced political smile on his face. He clasps my hand but doesn't let go. "Samantha Alistair Brooks. Daughter of the diplomat?"

I don't like his clammy grip, but I can't break free. Not without causing a fuss in front of the entire graduating class and their parents. "Yes, sir," I say, keeping my eyes averted. *Don't hold up the line,* I urge him silently, hoping that his sense of propriety won't prolong the conversation.

"A good man," he says, keeping hold on me. "A patriot. It was a great loss to the country when he passed away. A heart attack, was it?"

"Yes, sir." I don't mention that his death was seen as suspicious at the time. Secret Service conducted an investigation, but nothing was conclusive. Or at least, nothing they told his twelve-year-old daughter.

"Didn't he have a son, as well?"

I glance back at Liam. He's taken two steps forward, and I know I only have to give him the signal and he'll barge onto the stage to remove the senator's hand from me. A short shake of my head. I can handle this myself. As he pointed out, I'll be on my own during the tour—and for the years to follow. My chest feels impossibly full at the thought.

Graduation should feel like a time of possibility, a time of hope. It makes me ache that my independence will come at such a steep price, distance from the man who's my only home.

"We aren't close," I say, which is an understatement. I haven't seen my brother since the last time he fought with my father and left. He's been in the military, though I suppose I wouldn't know if he got out. He declined to take custody of me when my father died. And he never reached out to me after that.

"A shame," the man says, still studying me.

I yank my hand back, the action sudden enough that he lets go of me. There's a residue of slickness left on my palm from the encounter, and I wipe my hand surreptitiously on my black gown. Perhaps my actions would be rude, but I think the senator was rude to detain me against my will.

There's another hour before the ceremony ends, during which time I can only play with the edges of the rolled diploma and the heavy satin ribbon that holds it.

When the principal finally calls an end to the proceedings, the parents surge forward in an enthusiastic rush. There are flowers and cards and balloons for the new graduates.

It's hard to see anything through the crowd of people. When I finally scoot my way to the back of the room, it's empty. I glance toward the stage, uncertain. Did he push inside the mass toward me? No, because if he had done that, he would have found me.

Which can only mean one thing—he left.

My stomach turns over. There are hundreds of people in the small auditorium, but I've never felt so alone. I can see Cody congratulating Laney across the room, but I don't want to answer questions about why Liam left early. And the last thing I want to do is be caught by the senator for more questions. I step into the hallway, which is abruptly empty, no one slamming lockers or dashing toward their classes.

That part of my life is over now.

I wander down the hallway, wondering if he's waiting for me by the car. For all I know he already left to go back to the house. It was Cody who dropped me and Laney off this morning. I'm sure he's willing to drive us back home, but the thought of Liam leaving without me makes my eyes burn.

Something slows my steps in front of the library, an unnatural awareness.

That's where I find him, amid the dusty shelves and walnut study tables. He stands by the large globe that serves as the library's centerpiece. It has three ornate iron feet to carry its weight, and two circumferences of wood that hold it in place. The surface of the water is smooth, and I know from memory, cool to the touch—made of stone, ironically. The land rises in uneven terrain, made from dark metal. He studies the staggering mass of North America, hands behind his back.

I come to him from behind. As far as I can tell, I haven't made a sound, but he can sense my presence.

"Congratulations," he says without turning.

"Thank you," I say, feeling cautious. There's a strange energy in the room, a kind of electric current, as if a thousand bolts of lightning spread out in infinite fractals, Liam at the center of the storm.

He reaches toward the globe. The blunt of his finger brushes Tanglewood, which is only a few hours from where we're standing. And the place where the tour will begin. "In a few months you'll be here. Practicing with Harry March. Performing in front of thousands of people."

My throat clenches around anxiety—and around grief. I'll start my life in Tanglewood, but before that I'll have to say goodbye to the one I have now. No matter where I go in the world, Liam will be here running North Security.

"Will you miss me?" I venture to ask.

He moves his finger up to New York City, where we'll play Carnegie Hall, one of the most prestigious venues for classical music. Rumor is that a pedestrian on Fifty-seventh Street, Manhattan, stopped the violinist and composer Heifetz and inquired, *Could you tell me how to get to Carnegie Hall?*

Yes, said Heifetz. *Practice!*

The story has become part of the lore around

Carnegie Hall—and around classical music itself. All that practice must have paid off, because I'm heading there. It will be the culmination of a dream.

And the end of a childhood marked by loneliness and tenuous hope.

Hope that came from Liam North.

"Miss you?" he says, almost tasting the words, as if they're foreign to him. Maybe for a man like him they are foreign, the whole idea of needing someone else. Of longing for them. He's so strong. So self-contained. Is that something I'll find as I get older? Or is it unique to him, forever out of my reach?

His hand falls away, and I replace it with mine, touching New York City and then Boston and then Chicago. Vancouver and then Seattle. Los Angeles. That will be the last stop on the US tour.

I lift my finger so it hovers over the globe, the metal landscape apart from me.

Liam spins the globe lightly, until I'm holding my finger over Tokyo. The first stop on the Asia tour. Then there will be the European tour. And South America.

A major record label put together the tour. They're going to record the first concert, the one in Tanglewood, and release it as an album titled *Concerto*. Its release will be staggered across the globe to coincide with our tour.

"I won't miss you," he says, his tone soft and final.

My breath catches. *Don't cry,* I order myself. I swallow down the lump in my throat. Is there something wrong with me? Am I inherently unlovable? "I'll miss you," I say, not caring if it makes me weak.

"I *can't* miss you," he says, placing his hand over mine, moving our fingers back to the hill country of Texas, where Kingston nestles among the land and the lakes. "I wouldn't survive it."

"I'll come back," I promise, breathless. "After the tour. I'll visit—"

"Do you want to kill me, Samantha?"

I break off, uncertain whether he wants me to leave or stay here forever. Not knowing whether he hates me or loves me. "I want to please you."

"Then go away from here. Leave and don't come back."

CHAPTER NINETEEN

The most expensive opera costume of all time was worn by Adelina Patti at Covent Garden in 1895. It was worth £15 million.

SAMANTHA

A ROW OF shops along South Congress carry only the unique and eclectic and antique. There's a flower shop with a sofa and chair and coffee table molded from the ground and then grown over with super soft grass. An old record shop with cats that sleep in the dusty trays, shooting a dirty look if you try to shift the vinyl around them.

A whimsical toy shop that sells an action figure of Jane Austen.

Our goal is a large vintage clothing shop that takes up three stories. It's the kind of place where you have to look through a hundred racks of clothing to find one thing to buy. The smell of mothballs and incense fills the air. I didn't really feel like shopping, but poor Laney needs the distraction. Her mother has been gone a long time, and even for the daughter of a mercenary, someone used to absences, she must be getting nervous.

And maybe I'll find something special to wear on the tour.

Laney holds up a bright purple dress with puffy sleeves that could only have come from the eighties. "What do you think? It would be like that girl from *Charlie and the Chocolate Factory*, except instead of a giant blueberry I could be a giant grape."

"Knowing you, you'd probably bring the style back."

She shudders in mock agreement and shoves the dress back onto the rack. "You're probably right." After a short pause of moving hangers, she sighs. "I wish I could actually see the clothes that are right in front of me, but my mind keeps wandering. Next thing I know I'm looking at a lace cocktail dress in army green."

"Oh, that sounds nice actually," I say, peering around the thick rack of clothes. She swats me away, determined as ever to make me wear something that will actually attract attention instead of hide me. "Did you talk to Liam about it?"

"Yes," she says glumly. "He says they're safe and sound in Germany, resting before they come back. That's what he said—resting. Like what, are they taking a nap or something?"

"I'm sure they have a good reason," I say, keeping my voice free of the worry twisting my stomach. I'm not sure how she's managed to stay as calm and cool, but then again, she's had plenty of practice.

"Of course they have a good reason," she says. "Like the fact that they're *not* safe and sound. How do we feel about plaid? I mean in a short skirt—obviously yes. But what about this beret?"

I give her a dubious look. "Where would you wear a beret?"

"In Paris, when I have a torrid love affair with a moody musician. Oh by the way, I'm going to need you to introduce me to some moody musicians."

"Okay, well, first I'll have to meet some myself."

"You'll meet *plenty* on the tour. Starting with Harry March."

I make a face. "He's probably not even going to talk to me. I'll be like the stagehand, except less important, because I won't know where his microphone is."

"Whatever. You're going to wear something fabulous and you're going to play that way you do where everyone starts crying, and then he's going to fall madly in love with you."

"Speaking of madly in love, how is Cody?"

"Why would *that* be speaking of madly in love?"

Because he's been in love with Laney since they were children. "No reason."

She sighs. "He's glad that Coach Price is gone, obviously. But he didn't exactly bounce back from the experience. The school counselor tried to talk to him, but he shut her down."

"I'm sorry," I say, squeezing her hand. "He'll work through it in his own time."

"But my timeline is so much faster," she says, plaintive.

My hands pause in their path through the clothes. I pull out the black dress, a flush warming me. The fabric hangs awkwardly on the hanger, but there's something about it…

I wander over to one of the standing mirrors and hold the gown against me. It's an asymmetrical line, sloping down across my body. Ruffles of black silk line the top. It's simple and dramatic all at once, and the way it's cut will emphasize the violin I'll hold. It falls to the floor, approximating the more formal gown that a classical musician would wear, but with a high slit, befitting a popular music stage.

"Perfect," Laney breathes. "You have to get it."

"For the tour, right?"

"Well, sure, but you should wear it where Liam can see you. Maybe tomorrow."

Tomorrow is my birthday. Which means that at midnight Liam North will cease to be my court-ordered guardian. I make a face, trying to act like it's no big deal. "We don't have any big plans."

There's a pang in my chest, because we usually do something for my birthday. A nice dinner at the country club in Kingston or the latest hipster foodie restaurant in Austin. Liam will hand me a birthday card that's completely impersonal, in which he's signed his name—that's it.

We've done it for the past six years, so I just assumed… well, I suppose he doesn't owe me that. After all he's done, he doesn't owe me anything.

"Hey," Laney says, hugging me from behind. She gives me a small smile in the mirror. "Everyone is safe and sound, remember? They're only taking a nap."

I force a smile. "Of course they are. So let's pick out something for you. You *are* going to come to the opening night, aren't you? I'll have the moody musicians all lined up to meet you."

We look through racks for a few minutes, getting separated in the maze of old clothes, only the sound of hangers scraping across metal filling the air.

A sound comes from behind me, and I whirl, looking at the sea of colors, a thousand different fabrics and colors. *It would be so easy to hide in here.* The thought whispers through my brain. My heart pounds, and I take a step back.

Footsteps land heavy on the stairs, coming up toward us. For a second I think we're under attack, that someone dangerous is here.

Josh appears at the top of the stairs. "You girls ready?"

My breath still comes fast as I stare at him. I glance over my shoulder, but the riot of fabric looks the same. I must have imagined it. Living in the headquarters of North Security has probably made me paranoid. We check out at the registers downstairs.

As we get into Josh's truck, I glance at the upstairs window, where it looks like a shadow moves. Unease floods through my veins in staccato.

CHAPTER TWENTY

Before the nineteenth century, the violin bow was shaped like a hunting bow.

LIAM

MOONLIGHT STREAMS THROUGH the open window. Something must have woken me up. I check my phone, but there are no missed calls. It could have been a nightmare. Then I hear the strains of the violin drift through the crack in the door. I double-check the time.

Ten minutes to midnight.

She's only my ward for another ten minutes. Christ.

I pull on some jeans and head toward the music, not sure what I'll say when I get there. She used to wake up in the middle of the night to play, when she first got here. There was no sense of a normal schedule for her. She ate and slept and breathed on her father's wishes. I tried to instill a sense of normalcy, tried to show her what it was like to have a stable home, tried to… oh hell, whatever I tried, that's over now.

She usually wears her school uniform when she plays. Or jeans and a T-shirt. Something comfortable to last the hours she'll sit in roughly the same position.

But she's not wearing anything like that now.

Instead she's in a black dress that I've never seen before. My throat goes dry. She looks like someone else, like a grown woman. A sensual woman.

My body reacts suddenly, violently.

I force myself to walk into the room, to pretend like this is a thousand other times from the past, that she's still a child and I'm her guardian. Even though the seconds tick away with every breath.

"What's that?" I crouch down in front of her.

There are fifteen major violin scales. An almost infinite number of concertos and sonatas. I know almost all of them by heart. They are embedded into my skin, etched deeper with every afternoon of careful practice.

This one I don't recognize.

A blush steals over her cheeks. "Nothing."

The dress has a high slit, exposing one perfectly shaped leg. It would be so easy to push her knee open, to draw my fingers up the inside of her thigh. I rest my hand on her other knee, the one that's covered by black silky fabric.

"It's beautiful." *And haunting.*

"I'm only playing around," she says, her voice wavering.

"You're composing?" That's not something she's ever told me about. To play with her skill is a form of composition. She lends her interpretation to every piece—her passion, her heart. There is no such thing as a rote recitation for a prodigy like her.

Even so, writing her own composition would be something new.

"It's no big deal," she says quickly, giving a little shrug that moves the ruffles that lie against her breast, drawing my attention to the gentle curve.

"Where'd you get this?" I ask, keeping my voice even.

She didn't mean to kill me with this dress.

She doesn't mean to torture me, I'm almost sure.

"A vintage shop," she says, sounding shy. Maybe she *does* mean to torture me. "I thought I could wear it on the tour. What do you think? Should I?"

The thought of thousands of men seeing her

in this dress makes me want to lock her away. She would be terrified if she knew everything I think about. I can imagine her tied down on my bed wearing this dress, unable to get away from me, unable to do anything but take me. *Fuck.*

"Perhaps," I say, my tone noncommittal.

Disappointment flits across her pretty features. "Well, it's not decided or anything. There's still time to look. I just thought I'd try to play while I'm wearing it."

Christ. She deserves more than a surly bastard more concerned about his unholy obsession than her feelings. "You look beautiful, Samantha. You look…" I swallow hard. "You look like the most perfect woman I've ever seen. But I don't think it's the dress. It's you."

I've knelt down in front of her a thousand times before, but she's never been in a dress like this. And I've never been shirtless, my feet bare.

"Is that the only reason you're up this late? To try on the dress?"

A blush creeps up her cheeks, the soft line of her neck. The tops of her breasts, plump and gently sloping above the black ruffles. "I couldn't sleep, knowing that I turn eighteen soon."

"In about five minutes."

Emotions chase across her face, as clear as the

notes she plays on her violin—excitement, apprehension, a tentative hope. "I guess you must be relieved. Your civic responsibility will be over soon."

"Were you listening outside the door, Samantha?"

A soft laugh. "Guilty."

How can I resist her? The girl was beautiful and strong. The woman is devastating. "I do feel responsibility for you, but it has nothing to do with civic duty."

"Then why did you say that to the reporter?"

"I wanted her to leave it alone. And I didn't want to tell the real reason." I can't resist the truth when she's looking at me like that, her eyes liquid brown, full of desire. It makes me want to be the man she thinks I am—the one who could cherish and keep her. Have her and hold her. That man will never be me, but doesn't she deserve to know?

Or maybe I want one night of truth.

"What was the real reason?"

"That I loved you as soon as I heard you play. That I saw the way your father left you to fend for yourself, well before he died. That I wanted to hide you away from the world that would hurt you and scare you and use you, and I was just selfish enough to actually do it."

Her eyes widen. "You never said you loved me before."

"Love isn't something I ever wanted, Samantha. Especially parental love. That was the worst kind of all. It was dangerous. Cruel. I never wanted to do that to you."

It's more than I meant to give away, revealing what I think about parental love, how horrible it can be. She doesn't miss the implication. Her brown eyes widen. "What did your parents do to you?"

Once a principal had called my father. *This is incredible news,* the woman had said. *Your son is extremely gifted.* I spent three days and three nights in the well because of those test scores. I learned to get the answer wrong enough times not to attract attention, after that.

I never really believed the devil lived inside me. If I believed in the devil, then I had to believe in God, and he had abandoned me too long ago for me to speak his name—even to myself. It wasn't the devil, precisely. It was me. Simply me. As I'd traced my fingers along the moss-damp bottom of the well, I knew that I deserved to be down here. That every glimpse of sunlight was a gift I didn't deserve.

That every sweet thing I'd ever have would

have to be stolen.

"And then when that love started to change into something else, when it was spiked with desire, I didn't know how to handle that. It was better and so much worse at the same time."

"You don't have to be afraid of it."

"I'm not afraid."

"Maybe it's time that I gave you the sex talk," she says, her tone impish. "So that way you'll know what you're doing. Repeat after me: condoms are mandatory."

A bark of laughter escapes me. "I never stood a chance against you, did I?"

Her humor fades. "You've done a pretty good job resisting this."

Part of me still wants to deny it. Stubborn to a fault, that's me. But I can't pretend not to want her anymore. Lust thrums through my body in visible shudders. Being this close to her, touching her, but not having her—it's enough to rip me to shreds. "I shouldn't have kissed you."

"How much longer?" she whispers.

My internal clock is accurate down to the second. "A minute."

"What would you do to me? If I were over eighteen?"

Heat races through my veins. "I shouldn't

have kissed you, but I would do it again. And again. And again until you moaned into my mouth. And then I'd move lower, down your body. To your shoulders and your stomach. Your breasts. It's all I can think about."

Her chest rises and falls with rapid breaths. "Keep going."

How did I ever think I was the one with control in this relationship? Because I made rules and she followed them, but that was always her choice. I only ever had as much control as she gave me. And I'm helpless in the face of her desire. "I want to kiss you between your legs, to taste you, to drink you in and make you push your hips against my face. And all the while you'll play the violin, so perfect, so perfect, because you don't know how to make a mistake, not even if you tried."

Her eyes are wide and dark and luminous. "*Liam.*"

"But then I would find your clit. It would already be hard and throbbing. Slick. I'd flick it with my tongue, again and again, ruthless, not caring that you'd beg me to go slower or softer. Your hands would falter, and there would be a terrible sound from the violin, because you would come hard enough to forget."

"How much longer?" she says on a tortured

breath.

At some point my words stopped being hypothetical. They became a promise, and every muscle in me strains for completion. My whole body aches to hear the beautiful sounds as she rises and the terrible screech as she comes for me.

"Almost doesn't count," I mutter, grim and aching.

"Now."

I shake my head, my eyes not leaving hers. She's heavy-lidded, her lips gently parted. "Ten," I tell her. "Nine. Eight."

She moves her violin back into place, her arms up as the bow goes into position. How many times have I seen her like this? And yet she's completely different. It can't be the seconds ticking away. Nothing as external as time. Something's changed inside her.

"Seven. Six. Five."

The first note enters the air around us, and I feel it deep inside my body. In my muscle and bone. In my cock, which pushes against the rough denim of my jeans.

There is more than welcome in her eyes. There's challenge.

OVERTURE

SAMANTHA

I DON'T EXPECT him to actually touch me. "Four," he says, and I begin the opening rise of Beethoven's "5 Secrets." They're moving and sweet, with a touch of melancholy.

His eyes flicker with a deep shame. He doesn't want to want me, which is what makes it so sad. The music is how I speak to him. It's how he speaks back to me, his head bowed before me. Does it really matter so much whether I'm seventeen or eighteen? Does it really matter that a piece of paper makes him my guardian? He does not have a monopoly on being protective. It's not only him who decides what happens here.

I want to guard him from the onyx shadows in his green eyes.

"Three," he murmurs, and I expect him to walk away.

The bow moves almost on its own, my limbs forming around the instrument the way it wants. It's a sensual experience, playing the violin. I didn't realize how much until now.

He touches my lips with his thumb, the movement bold. His hand trails lower, over the shape of my breasts and the concave of my stomach.

"Two," he says, pushing my legs. The backs of

his knuckles brush the insides of my thighs, and everything in me tightens. Muscle memory is a powerful thing, and I manage to keep playing without missing a single note. Two fingers slip beneath the slit of the dress. Those green eyes widen, and I know he's shocked that I'm not wearing anything underneath.

My regular panties left an obvious line in the thin fabric of the dress. I'll need something else to wear underneath—a thong. Though at the moment having nothing feels more right than anything I could buy at a store.

"One," he says, his voice almost sympathetic. Rough finger pads open my most private place, searching and inexorable. I've never felt so exposed, even with nothing bared to his sight.

The hard part isn't playing the notes. It's keeping the tempo the same. My hands want to speed up, my body moving toward an uncertain peak. He finds a well of moisture and draws it up, his forefinger circling my clit. My breath shudders out of me.

"Keep playing," he murmurs, his thumb moving to my clit, his fingers searching below.

My eyes fall shut, but my hands know what to do even without watching. The bow meets the strings in perfect accord, the tempo rising only slightly. "Don't stop," I say on a moan.

A humorless huff of laughter. "I couldn't."

His hands move with startling knowledge of my body, as if he's been practicing for ten thousand hours, as if I'm his instrument to play. Pleasure swirls inside me, soft at first, and then louder, unmistakable. Orgasm wrenches my body with sudden violence.

A loud screech rents the air as my bow rubs discordant against the strings.

In the aftermath of my climax, Liam gently strokes the inside of my thigh. My body twitches and sighs, struggling for equilibrium. I open my eyes to find him watching me.

"You stopped playing," he says, his tone grave, a hint of erotic playfulness lurking deep in those moss-green eyes. "We'll have to start over again. And again. Until you get it right."

"Oh no," I protest weakly, not sure my body can take another ounce of pleasure.

"Oh yes," he says, a note of mock regret in his voice. "Practice makes perfect."

My limbs feel like they're made of jelly as I play the opening rise of Beethoven's "5 Secrets" again. Liam's fingers work with devastating accuracy to bring me to the peak. I tighten my hold on the neck of the violin, determined to finish this time, to play the song to completion.

Then he spreads my legs wider and presses his mouth to my core, and I'm lost.

LIAM

I REST MY forehead against the inside of her thigh, breathing roughly, struggling to control the lust raging in my veins. My lips feel swollen from kissing her. The scent of her arousal engraves my memory for safekeeping. There will be no time when I don't think of this night, when it doesn't make me hard. When I don't wish I could do it again.

Samantha makes little whimpers, as if it's too much, as if she's oversensitive even though I'm not touching her anymore. There's no way she can know how the sounds incense me, how I want to make her come again just to prove that she can take more. I'll show her, I'll *make* her. Some shred of reason holds me back. Perhaps the certainty that I would not be able to keep from fucking her if I heard her come again, if I felt her liquid on my lips, her secret muscles clenching my tongue as if they could draw it inside her body.

"God," she says, sounding shattered. Sounding broken.

I did that to her.

The irony rises over me, a shadow with weight, a goddamn cross to bear. *God,* she says again, but it doesn't have anything to do with a divine being. It's the other guy. The one who's always been inside me. By touching Samantha, I finally proved my father right. The devil lives inside me. Doesn't he? And the worst part, the truly unforgivable part, is that I would do it again. Now that I know Samantha's intimate flavor I can't imagine not knowing. It seems like not breathing. Not living. And I'd gave up any miniscule chance at redemption to have it.

"Go to bed," I say, hoarse from the restraint it takes to not bear her down on the floor and invade her body like an animal, in full view of her violin and my office. These symbols of my guardianship and her childhood made witness. "It's late."

I move to stand up, but her hand touches my cock. It just reaches out and lands on my cock, only denim and cotton separating her flesh from mine. A wave of desire overtakes me, and the only thing I can do is freeze.

"Let me," she says, still breathless, almost begging. "Let me touch you."

"No." The word comes out like a slap, and

she flinches.

"I want to please you."

There is no hell that would be deep enough, hot enough, painful enough for me. "I took advantage of you. And now you want to please me?"

Anger shoulders aside the lust in her eyes. "You took advantage of me? No, Liam. I made this decision."

"Really? You put on that dress because you wanted to make me insane with desire? You wore no panties so I wouldn't rip them to shreds? You spread your legs because you knew I would eat you like a madman?" She looks so beautiful as she comes. Her hoarse cries are sweeter music than anything her violin could produce. She's everything good and pure and right in this world, and all I can think about is defiling her again.

Her cheeks turn pink. "I didn't plan this, but I chose it all the same. I could have said no."

"It wouldn't have stopped me."

"Liar," she says, softly, almost sadly. "You didn't take advantage of me, and you couldn't hurt me if you tried. Not like this. You hurt me in other ways. By telling me that you don't want a relationship after the tour. That you don't love me. I love you, you know that? I do, but you don't care. You're too busy fighting with your demons."

"I'm not fighting demons, sweetheart. I am one."

Her eyes are wide and luminous. "You really believe that, don't you?" she says, her voice wondering. "Why do you believe that?"

With a growl I push away from her, pacing across the parquet floor, damning the iron-hard erection in my jeans. "If you knew the number of people I killed you wouldn't ask that."

"Almost everyone on your payroll is ex-military," she says in an outrageously reasonable tone. "Do you think they're bad people?"

"Of course not."

"Then what makes you different?"

I can't possibly explain all the deep-rooted ways. When you grow up with abusive parents you either hate the world or you find a way to rationalize their behavior. You think, maybe they're right. Maybe they see something in me that's fundamentally flawed. Maybe I should drink dirty well water to survive, only to throw it back up, and then stew in it for the next twenty-four hours before my father sends the rope down. Samantha knows something about shitty parents, but she doesn't know my secrets—and God willing she never will.

That's how I leave her, collapsed on her practice chair, boneless with satiated desire, hurt a clear bell in her eyes.

CHAPTER TWENTY-ONE

The most expensive violin ever sold cost $16 million.

SAMANTHA

WHEN I WAKE up in the morning, I'm back in my bed, Liam nowhere to be seen. I don't feel one year older or one day older. I'm a million years older, not because of the clock ticking away—but because of what happened with Liam last night. I examine myself in the mirror—the same brown eyes and brown hair. The same slight build that by some quirk of nature gave me the ability to play the violin with a speed and grace that astonished kings. Well, so much for being a child prodigy. It's my eighteenth birthday.

I'm not a child any longer.

Liam North doesn't have custody of me anymore.

The knowledge should give me a sense of independence, of grief. Of power and loss in equal measure. For surely I've lost as much as I've gained as the calendar flicked past yesterday. I don't feel any of those things, only a curious hollowness. Maybe I'm in a kind of emotional shock, my body resorting to numbness in order to avoid the pain.

There is only one thing that could possibly cut through the gauzy material that separates me from reality right now. The same thing that has always helped me hurt and heal, the lodestone of all my emotion. And that's music. After a quick shower I make my way downstairs.

Standing in the doorway, I know immediately that something is different.

That something is wrong.

The violin I've used for the past five years is a lovely Nicolo Amati, its bearing proud, its sound clear. There are multiple cracks that have been professionally repaired. It is on the whole weatherworn and discolored, the pedigree exceeding its appearance.

Even in its shabby state it's worth several hundred thousand dollars at auction—and of course, like most other things in my possession, it does not actually belong to me. It's owned by Liam North, purchased by him, his name on the insurance papers. It sleeps in a thoroughly modern suspension case made of carbon fiber. There could be a nuclear disaster, and the violin would remain inside the rectangular case, fully protected and encased in microfiber.

Gone.

The carbon fiber case, the Nicolo Amati violin. All of it, gone.

There is my chair with faded fabric and gleaming wood, the one I usually use to practice. My stand. The sheets of music that I'm practicing for the tour.

"A birthday gift," comes a low voice from behind me. Liam moves so stealthy that I didn't hear him. "We still have the Amati, if you want to keep it."

I take a step closer, examining the case, which is clearly an antique in its own right, with its smooth satinwood surface and brass closures. Even a few feet away I can feel the presence of the violin inside, as if its heartbeat thrums through the case.

He said I could keep the Amati, but it isn't really mine.

"I—don't understand." Violins like this aren't gifts. They are sold at auction, usually to museums and societies. Occasionally to eccentric billionaires with more money than musical skill.

"I had a hell of a time tracking down the owner after the last auction. He preferred to remain anonymous, but I promised him—well, more money than he can spend in his lifetime. And a private demonstration at its debut in Tanglewood by the famous violin prodigy Samantha Brooks."

A brass lock plate is engraved with the following words: *Lady Tennant/40 Grosvenor Square W.*

"Oh my God," I whisper.

"We can get a new case," he says, sounding gruff and strangely uncertain. "One with your name on it. This is the one it came with."

"Don't you dare," I say, half laughing, half crying.

There are only five hundred Stradivarius violins left in the world. Even so there are too many for me to know the provenance of every single one, but I know this one. *Lady Tennant* got its name because it was purchased by Sir Charles Tennant as a gift for his wife.

My hands are shaking as I reach for the clasps and open the case. I barely feel worthy to touch this violin—and I can't even imagine owning it, even though that's apparently what's just happened. I grasp the violin gently by its neck, lifting it from the case, and all my tremors evaporate. It's like the part in Harry Potter where the wand chooses the wizard. In this case it's the violin choosing me.

I'm tempted to run my fingertips over the strings and the neck, to learn its terrain by touch. But a violin's imperative is to play, and so I lift the bow and touch it to the strings. The sound soars through the air, the clearest note I've ever heard.

An opening scale and it sounds as momentous and poignant as any classical piece. It feels like I'm playing violin for the first time, hearing notes in an entirely new way.

I look back at Liam. He's always appreciated my playing. I suppose he would have gone mad by now if he didn't, having my music room connected to his office. Even he looks awed by the sound.

"How did you know?" I murmur, reluctant to set down the violin for even one moment.

"You like it?" His voice is roughened with something, maybe emotion. Are the strings of a Stradivarius so compelling that they'll move a man of strength and stoicism to this?

"It's the best thing anyone's ever done for me. More than I ever imagined." And then it doesn't matter how much I long to hold Lady Tennant or play everything I've learned with her—I have to set her gently into the case. That's where my carefulness ends.

I launch myself at Liam, throwing my arms around his neck and squeezing. There's moisture where my cheek touches his hard jaw, and I know he'll be embarrassed by my wild show of gratitude. He's never liked me being overly emotional, so I've tried so hard to be like him.

When I pull back, his green eyes shine with what can only be tears. It's enough to make my breath catch. Maybe he isn't as stoic as he wants me to think.

Maybe we're more alike than I ever knew.

In the moments that follow I become aware that I'm clinging to him like I'm drowning and he's my last chance of survival. Sensation blooms in my chest, my belly, and lower, to where my legs are half wrapped around him. He releases me gently, and I slide down his body to the floor.

"I'm old enough," I whisper, because it means he doesn't have to hold himself back from me. He doesn't have to feel bad about the erection I can feel cradled between our bodies.

He looks more torn than ever, shame hard in his eyes, his mouth a firm line. "The violin, Samantha. It was more than a birthday present. It's a goodbye."

CHAPTER TWENTY-TWO

In comparison to many other instruments, the piano is relatively new. It was invented in 1698 by Bartolomeo Cristofori in Italy.

SAMANTHA

BEA CALLS ME that afternoon, launching into an a cappella rendition of "Happy Birthday" with her husky, show tunes voice as soon as I say hello.

I grin at her on FaceTime. "You should give up the whole piano thing," I tell her. "Or at the very least become the next Adele."

"We'll call that plan B," she says, laughing.

"You won't believe what happened this morning."

"Ooh, something fun, I hope."

"I still can't even believe it, and I was there." I've got Lady Tennant in my lap, stroking the wood. I haven't been able to let go of it, actually. When I'm not playing it, I'm holding it.

"Now you're just teasing me. What happened?"

"Liam got me a Strad," I tell her, unable to hold back the squeal. A professional violinist may go through a few violins in their lifetime, on the quest to find the perfect one. Other times it comes to you early.

"Oh. My. God."

"The Lady Tennant." It's incredible to be able to share this with another musician. She's not a violinist, but she understands the power of a premier instrument—especially one with history.

"The Lady Tennant?" she says, sounding awed.

"He bought it. Outright. And then gave it to me. Honestly I might throw up."

"Well, don't throw up on a Stradivarius or you'll probably lose your violin license."

"I can't put it down. Like honestly, it's been hours. I can't let go of it."

"Of course you can't let go of it. It's your baby now. What are you just going to put it back in its case? How will it know how much you love it?" She's teasing me, in the way where she fully understands why I can't let go of it.

I'm in my bedroom now, and I gently nudge the door shut so I can say what's on my mind. "Actually, the violin is more than a birthday present. It's a goodbye present."

A pause. "What does that mean?"

Grief lances my heart, but I try for a matter-of-fact tone. "I guess it means I'm not going to see Liam again after I leave for the tour. That's probably for the best. It's not like we're family."

"Wow," she says, falling silent again.

"Wow what?"

"That's both incredibly generous and incredibly cold."

"No, it's—" My throat tightens. "He doesn't owe me anything. He certainly didn't owe me this violin. It shows how much he understands me. How much he cares for me."

"Yes," she says drily. "So much that he doesn't want to see you again."

Tears prick my eyes like hot pokers. "He's always been a realist."

"He's always been an asshole," she says with a sigh. "But you love him."

Yes, but not the way she means. Not as a father. I love him as more than that—as my everything. "You don't keep in touch with Edward," I say, trying to sound reasonable. We had that in common, guardians who cared for us out of obligation rather than familial love.

"Because I didn't love Edward. And he didn't

love me."

"There. You see? Exactly like me and Liam."

"It's the exact opposite of you and Liam, Samantha. You love him. And he feels something for you. Why do you think I called him an asshole?"

"Because he wanted me to go to high school instead of tour professionally?"

"No, he was probably right about that. I thought he was an asshole because he keeps his distance from you instead of saying how he really feels."

My body tightens as I remember his hands on my thighs, his tongue on my clit. "What if the way he feels about me isn't appropriate for a guardian to his ward?"

"He isn't a regular guardian," she says gently. "And you aren't a regular ward. So why should your feelings be the same as other people?"

"Beatrix, whatever happened between you and Edward?" He was her father's business partner. When both her parents died, he became the trustee of the considerable wealth she inherited. The only thing I know is that they had a falling out about her husband.

"He wanted to marry me," she admits. "Not in the sweet 'I love you' way. More like a 'you can't leave the penthouse so you'll make a nice attic wife for me' way."

"Oh, Bea. Why didn't you tell me?"

"I was embarrassed. Ashamed, really. I didn't have a regular life going to high school. You know I couldn't even leave the hotel for years, until I met Hugo."

"Edward didn't take it well?"

"No, and there's something else, something I found out about his past. It doesn't matter now except to say that he's not a good man."

My heart clenches. "I'm sorry."

"I know we have this in common, and I'm grateful to call you my friend. But our situations are completely different. Even before I knew the truth about Edward, I knew I couldn't marry him. That I would never love him—not as a husband or as a guardian."

She's right. Our situations aren't the same at all. If Liam North were to ask me to marry him, I would give up everything to say yes. The tour, a music career. Traveling the world. I'm excited about it, but it pales in comparison to the man one floor down. Of course, he would never ask me to marry him. He doesn't even want to see me again. I stroke the smooth wood of the Stradivarius, which may be all I ever have of Liam North.

CHAPTER TWENTY-THREE

The world's fastest violinist played "The Flight of the Bumblebee" averaging fifteen notes per second.

SAMANTHA

LANEY INSISTS ON taking me to the local café, where we have tea and chocolate croissants while discussing the latest *Outlander* episode. Josh drives us there, even securing the back exit before he lets us come inside. I give him a strange look. He's often been responsible for driving us around, the most overqualified chauffeur in the world, but this seems extreme.

In answer he gives me a wink and takes his latte outside.

I glance back at Laney, who's trying to hide her grin. And the notch of worry between her eyes is gone. "Do you have good news?" I demand, already suspecting as much.

A grin. "I wasn't supposed to tell you, but…my mom got back last night. She's exhausted but absolutely all in one piece. I checked. Two arms. Two legs. One nose. It's all there."

I give her a quick hug. "I'm so glad. But wait. Why were you not supposed to tell me?"

She rolls her eyes. "Because Elijah came back with her, and he's all like, 'I got Samantha a snow globe from the Kremlin and you can't tell her I'm here until I give it to her.'"

A bemused laugh escapes me. None of that sounds true. "Whatever."

"The important thing is that everyone is home. Nothing dangerous ever happens in Kingston."

I stick out my tongue at her. "Way to tempt fate."

An unrepentant grin. "Sorry, but I'm a firm believer in nihilism. We don't believe in fate, but we also think that if fate did exist, tempting it wouldn't matter. What's going to happen will happen."

"I'm pretty sure that's determinism."

"Exactly," she says, snatching the last bite of chocolate croissant from my plate. "Which means I'm not responsible for stealing this, and it doesn't matter anyway."

"You know what? I'm not even mad."

She grins. "Because you have a fancy new

violin waiting at home?"

"Yes." My smile fades. "Though it won't be home for long."

"Ugh. I can't believe he said that to you. Just do what I do when I don't like something—pretend it didn't happen. Show up whenever you want. What is he gonna do? Turn you away?"

My stomach turns over, despite the comforting tea and croissant I just ate. "Even if I can come back, that's going to be in a year and a half. And that's only the initial tour dates. If I get booked for concerts after that, it could be even longer."

The label will put me up in hotels for the tour. And after that? I'll basically be homeless. Oh, I'll have enough money to rent an apartment or something.

It won't really be a home.

Silence falls between us, both of us wondering where we'll be in two years from now. The future stretches out with endless uncertainty. Well, maybe I'm the only one wondering that. It's possible Laney's considering stealing the chocolate croissant from the display case.

After all, it would happen anyway.

A rap on the window. Josh taps his watch.

"Let's go," Laney says, grabbing her purse.

I take a final swallow of my tea. "Yeah, I've got to get my snow globe."

On the drive back to the house I notice Josh's raw knuckles.

"Who did you hit?" I say, disapproving. All three brothers are well trained and determined, but of the three of them, only Josh enjoys a fight.

"Oh, this?" he says, his tone innocent. "This was just a love tap."

He drops us off at the front of the house. It's dark and unnervingly quiet inside. I wonder if Liam is working, and if he'd mind if I played the Strad again.

"*Surprise!*"

A squeak escapes me as people jump out from behind the furniture and around the corner. My heart thumps in uneven rhythm. I grin at Laney with accusation. "Did you know about this?"

"It was my job to distract you."

"So sneaky," I say, looking around at the hot pink balloons and neon green streamers. A cake on the dining table forms the shape of a violin, the frosting in bright colors.

"I basically told you," she protests, laughing. "The snow globe. *The Kremlin.* Honestly who buys souvenirs from the Kremlin?"

"Those are the worst hints in the history of

the world." I throw my arms around her for a big hug. "And thank you for being an amazing friend."

It seems like all the people who work for North Security are in attendance, including Hassan and his young bride, back from their honeymoon and googly-eyed in love. There's Laney's mom, looking no worse for the wear. Liam, looking grave surrounded by so much revelry.

Elijah is back, and though he doesn't have a snow globe, he does have a black eye. I'm careful not to make a fuss over him in front of everyone—I know he'd hate that.

After "Happy Birthday" has been sung and the cake has been cut, I corner Elijah with a hug. He gives me a quick squeeze before letting me go. Strangely enough, Elijah is known as the asshole out of the three brothers, but my relationship with him has always been easiest. Maybe because we're closest in age or because you always know where you stand with him.

Though I think it's more likely because we both know about loss.

"I was worried about you," I tell him.

"You know I'm too stubborn to die. I'll probably live to be two hundred." He doesn't sound very cheerful about the prospect. But then again, he doesn't sound cheerful about much of anything.

I give a pointed look to his black eye. "You're not infallible."

"You should see the other guy."

"Nice try, but I already know Josh hit you. And he looks fine."

He grins, which with the black eye makes him look like a pirate. "And I'm guessing Liam will give me a matching one on the other side when he has a spare minute."

"Liam wouldn't hit you," I say, indignant. "You're injured."

"My pride is the only thing injured if you think I can't take a punch. Besides, I deserved it. I deserved worse than that, but Liam's gone soft."

"Because he cares about you."

Elijah studies me, his hard features set into shadows and edges. His face gives the impression of a cliff, something that's been hewn over centuries of water and wind but still manages to have hard angles. "No, squirt," he says gently. "It's because he cares about you. Everything changed the day he got custody of you."

I look away. Is that why he's so eager to get rid of me? I imagine a twelve-year-old girl would cramp anyone's style, especially a man in his prime who loves adventure. And women. My stomach clenches. "I suppose he'll join one of the teams once I'm gone."

"He doesn't want to do that shit anymore."

"Or maybe he just didn't go because he felt obligated to stay with me."

"He used to take any job. Every job. If it was likely to end up with him in a wooden box, he would do it. He wanted it to end that way. It was only his bad luck that kept him alive."

The way Elijah speaks, I know he's talking from experience. "Is that what you do?"

A humorless smile. "That's the North brothers' curse. To survive."

SAMANTHA

THE PARTY GOES late into the night. It's ten o'clock when Laney comes to me quietly. "Cody's here. He's outside. He doesn't want to come in."

The hair on the back of my neck rises at her tone. "What's going on?"

She glances to the large windows that overlook the hills. Any gathering here involves beer and an overabundance of testosterone, which led to the men competing in impromptu boxing matches. Liam was called outside to arbitrate a particularly dirty one.

Only his decisions are trusted as being completely impartial.

"He's got bruises," she whispers.

Birthday cake turns to lead in my stomach. Cody has always hidden his bruises from Liam—and usually from us. He must be in a bad way if he's come here. "Should I tell Liam?"

Her eyes widen. "You can't."

"He helped with Coach Price."

"That was different. He could get rid of Coach Price. How is he going to get rid of Cody's dad?"

"The authorities. A social worker. I don't know."

"The man's the only family Cody has. Do you think he's going to be safer in some group home? And besides, you had to convince Liam to help with Coach Price. What if he won't be convinced this time?"

For all I know there are a hundred Coach Prices working at the group home. And besides, I know what it's like to have a father who isn't very good—but he's the only one you have. I wouldn't want Cody to lose that—or to suffer retribution if his father finds out he talked to us.

"I still think we should tell Liam."

"We can talk about that later, but right now I'm going on a drive with him."

"Do you want me to come with you?"

"Maybe," she says. "No, it's your birthday party. Don't be silly."

"I'm not being silly. You guys are my best friends. If he needs to talk, I should be there." A thought occurs to me, and my cheeks heat. "Unless you'd rather be alone."

Shock widens her eyes. "Nothing like that is going to happen."

"Okay," I say, keeping my tone mild.

"I'm serious. Now you have to come."

She slips outside, and I start to follow. At the threshold of the house I pause, remembering the strange sounds and shadows in the antique shop. Probably my imagination.

"Come on," she says, and I take another step forward.

And then stop.

Your father had enemies. If they think you know something—

No, I won't leave without telling anyone where I'm going. Liam was right about that—it's not the grown-up decision to make people worry.

I find Liam outside, shaking his head as Josh

and Elijah fight across the grass, tumbling outside the makeshift white boundary, using moves that I'm pretty sure aren't allowed in even the most underground boxing ring.

"I'm going on a drive with Laney and Cody."

"No," he says, almost absently, his eyes still on the fight.

"I'm not asking permission," I tell him gently. "I'm eighteen now. Remember?"

He glances at me, his green eyes filled with humor and melancholy. "Would you have asked permission if I agreed to be pen pals when you left?"

I shake my head slowly, not breaking eye contact.

"Christ," he says. "All right. Go. I won't try to stop you, but I'm still responsible for your safety as long as I—as long as you're here. I'll follow at a discreet distance."

I make a face. "Are you serious?"

"Hey," he says gently. "I know how to tail someone without them knowing."

"That's weirdly reassuring."

That earns me a small smile.

Outside I find Cody and Laney waiting by the beat-up white truck, Cody looking miserable, his shoulders slumped as if perpetually protecting himself. He actually looks better than Elijah—no black eyes or visible bruises. I think they're all on his ribs. His father hits him where it can't be seen.

I move to hug him, but he takes a reflexive step back.

My face falls, but I struggle to act casual. "I heard we're going for a drive."

"Happy birthday," he says, apology in his voice. "I got you a present, but it's… I lost it."

More likely his father found it, whatever it was, and beat him for it. Acid rises in my throat. I hate not being able to do anything about it.

Maybe on the drive I can convince him Liam can help.

"The only thing I want for my birthday is hanging out with you," I say, climbing into the truck. I don't know how much a normal high school experience really helped me. The endless classes and exams when all I really wanted to do was play the violin. Having Laney and Cody as friends is different. If this is what normal means, I understand why it's so important.

I know without asking that we're heading to the lake, where trails lead to a rocky swimming hole. We go there a lot to hang out. Except we barely get ten minutes from home before headlights appear behind us, way too close to the truck. Cody swears in surprise. "What the hell?"

"Oh my God," I moan. "He said he would be discreet."

Laney turns in her seat. "I hate to be the bearer of bad news, but that's not anyone from North Security. It's a Crown Victoria, late nineties model."

She has that kind of detailed knowledge of random things, so I trust her. The North Security vehicles are all black Explorers designed to hold a maximum number of people, and a couple large trucks for hauling supplies.

"Then who is it?" Cody says as the car behind us speeds up.

Impact. We're jolted forward as the car slams into the truck. Cody swerves hard but manages to keep the truck on the road.

"No one we want to meet," I say, gripping the leather seat. "Keep going."

It comes to me with calm certainty—this is about my father.

A child who might remember something from when she was hiding under her father's desk. Not only from the day he died. From before that. A phone call. A conversation.

I still don't remember anything. There were diplomats and formal dinners where I would be forced to wear itchy dresses. Endless phone calls where I would play with my doll underneath his desk. *What could I have heard that's dangerous?* Maybe Liam is right. It doesn't matter what I've heard. It only matters that someone thinks I might know something.

The car behind us speeds up, pulling alongside. "Oh shit," Laney says.

They're trying to run us off the road. The crunch of metal. Cody fights to keep the truck straight. If we go off the road right now, we'll head straight into a ditch—and then be sitting ducks. Elijah taught me self-defense, but I have a feeling the man in that car has a gun.

A burst of light as a large black SUV jumps onto the road, headlights overbright, engine smooth and loud. It must be Liam in one of the Explorers. He slams into the Crown Vic, pushing it into the embankment instead of us.

Cody fights the steering, but we're going too fast. There's a loud *pop* as the ancient white pickup truck is pushed one mile past its endurance. The truck swerves hard, almost flipping over, before it rocks back onto four wheels.

There's a shout. A wild cry.

The whole world shakes as we leave the pavement and hit sliding rocks.

A tree looms ahead in the windshield. We're slowing down, but not fast enough. We slam into the trunk with a loud *thunk* and the punch of a half-inflated, ancient, yellowed airbag.

CHAPTER TWENTY-FOUR

The London Symphony Orchestra was booked to travel on the Titanic's maiden voyage, but they changed boats at the last minute.

LIAM

THE MAN DRIVING the Crown Victoria has pale eyes and a scar across his left eye. I put a bullet in the middle of his forehead before he can talk. There's a half second of regret about that. He could have had useful information, though probably not. And he deserved a painful death. But I can't risk the fucker hurting anyone while I'm losing my mind with worry. I sprint across the road to the white truck, which smokes from its rumpled hood. By the time I get there Cody is helping Laney out. Samantha pushes her way out from the other side, in time for me to catch her in my arms.

"Are you okay? Talk to me." I run my hands over her body, searching for injuries. The whole chase probably lasted two and a half seconds, but it's more than enough for someone to be hurt. For someone to be killed. The human body is so fucking fragile.

She pushes at my hands. "I'm fine. *Liam,* I'm fine."

I hold myself back long enough to study her face. Her brown eyes are wide with worry. Tear tracks glisten down her cheeks. "I'm not," I say hoarsely. "I'm not fucking fine."

Then I clutch her to my chest, trying in vain to control the wild beat of my heart. I feel like some kind of feral creature. I want to beat the earth and howl at the moon. I want to find the fuckers who sent an *assassin* after Samantha and rip them apart with my bare hands.

All I can do is stand here and hold her—and hold her. And hold her. It's woefully inadequate, but the alternative is to lose my fucking mind, and she needs me right now.

It feels like an eternity, the perfect clock in my head gone haywire. Three Explorers pull up, my brothers descending with harsh efficiency to handle the body, to check on Laney and Cody, to get the local law enforcement involved. That last one is a courtesy. We all know with grim and silent communication that we'll find the fuckers behind this and dispose of them ourselves.

Josh tries to take her from me. "I'm not sure she can breathe," he says.

Of course she can breathe. I have my hand on her back, feeling her lungs move. I've touched her pulse. Even the tears that dampen her lashes. I need to feel those signs of life.

Elijah shows up with a grim face. "No ID on the body. The tags are cut off his clothes. The VIN number filed off the car. The sheriff's going to call in the FBI on this."

Christ, this place was going to be a circus in a matter of minutes.

"I'm taking her back to the house. They can question us there once they've processed the scene."

"They aren't going to like the shooter leaving," Josh says, rueful.

"Wait," Samantha says, struggling to step back. "I'm not going to leave Laney and Cody here."

"They'll be safe," I say, lifting her body into the air and hauling her to the nearest company car. She gasps in shock, fighting me before I click the seat belt into place and shut the door. Her loyalty to her friends is admirable, but they have a goddamn army to protect them in case there are any more mercenaries lurking in these woods.

And I'm not going to leave Samantha exposed out here for one more second, not for anything, not when I feel her trembling in my arms.

When we get home, I carry her upstairs, even though she protests she can walk. I consider taking her to my room—I want her in my bed, where she'll be safe. And never leave.

Instead I force myself to carry her to her bedroom. I set her down on the warm tile of her bathroom floor as I turn the water to hot and fill the tub.

She works at the hem of her shirt, getting herself caught in the fabric. She's too worked up to undress herself—and so I'll do it for her. I unveil each inch of skin with undue care, mindful of bruises that might form in the next few hours, even days. Small quivers take her muscles, a reminder that she isn't as composed as she wants me to think.

This is the first time I've ever seen her fully naked.

Even with danger so nearby, my body reacts to hers with intense arousal. As I pull her panties down her legs, exposing her slender thighs and the dark curls between them, my cock reacts with a throb. I want the ultimate sign of life, her cunt pulsing around me, slick and warm and soft. She looks like a dream, full of rosy peach hues and creamy vanilla. There is no end to the places I want to taste her. I could make her stand in the foyer as a living statue. It's sick, the ways I want to see her, use her, the ideas her bare body gives me. Depraved.

Instead I help her into the bathtub, where I wash her with soap. Everywhere. Even when she blushes and murmurs in embarrassment, I slide the soap over her nipples and between her legs. Between the firm cheeks of her ass. There is a primal need inside me, to serve her, to care for her, and I'm as helpless to the urge as she is. She's Venus with her upturned breasts and demure pose. Her hair falling around her in erotic abandon. There's never been anything more beautiful than this. Enough to bring a man to his knees. Enough to make me wish I was anything other than her former guardian.

I use the peach-scented bottles to wash and shampoo her hair, my rough hands working carefully through the strands, making them lather and then cream and then clean again.

When she's dry, I tuck her into bed with its pale pink sheets and white lace coverlet, with the cream-colored throw pillow with a brown violin embroidered on it. God, she looks so vulnerable in that bed. So vulnerable and impossibly strong. The urge to hold her runs through me, a physical sensation that makes me tremble.

I turn to leave her, forcing myself to let her rest. She deserves that much.

"Don't go," she whispers.

The bed is twin-size, which isn't enough for the both of us. And it highlights how young she is, how wrong I was to ever let her climb into my king-size bed down the hall.

Shivers run through her, and I climb in behind her, pulling her close into the fortress of my body. My eyes are wide. Sleep will be impossible tonight. Tomorrow. Maybe ever. All I can do is watch over her. No one will touch her.

She drifts into a restless slumber, her body warm but still shivering.

SAMANTHA

LIAM WAKES ME up just before midnight, nudging me gently out of the hazy, dark sinkhole of dreams. It takes me a moment to remember that the crash wasn't only in my imagination. New twinges wake up throughout my body as I move to stand, and I can't hide a wince.

"Dr. Foster's downstairs," he says, a knowing

sympathy in his eyes. "And the police want to ask some questions. I've given them fifteen minutes. They know you need to sleep."

I manage a wry smile. "If a question gets too personal, you'll step in?"

He raises an eyebrow, bemused by my mood. I'm bemused, too. It's a strange thing to realize I miss his overprotective tendencies. Maybe that's how I truly know I've grown up—that I can long for the relative safety of my childhood with Liam North.

But the detectives are courteous and professional. Unlike the reporter, they haven't been digging into my personal background before they show up. They aren't aware there's any connection between my father and what happened tonight. *Did the driver interact with you before he rammed from behind? Do you know why he was chasing you?*

They show me a photo of him, leaning back in the driver's seat, a neat hole in the center of his forehead. I shiver, and Liam rubs slow circles on my back. *Have you seen him before?*

No, no, and no.

The doctor looks me over and declares me healthy—some bruising, he says, offering a prescription that is guaranteed to numb the pain.

"No," I say because I think the nightmares may be worse.

Liam accepts the bottle with a grim nod, keeping it safe in case I need it.

Then he takes me back upstairs and tucks me into bed. "What about Laney?" I ask, pain and adrenaline making me jittery. "What about Cody's truck? His dad—"

"I know," Liam says, his green eyes fathomless. "I'll take care of them."

"You said he's not your business."

"I was wrong, Samantha."

I clasp his wrist in a wordless plea, feeling the interplay of tendon and muscle, a silent string instrument in the form of a man.

He climbs into the bed behind me, his warmth an immediate comfort.

"You don't have to stay." I close my hand around his arm, pressing my fingers along the strings as if it were the neck of a violin—G4, D4, A4, E5.

He doesn't move, but I feel his gentle amusement ripple the air. "Let me," he murmurs. "After seeing the truck go off the road, I'm definitely going to have nightmares."

And I sink back into the murky sleep, the one with my father shouting, pleading, cursing.

CHAPTER TWENTY-FIVE

In addition to being a composer and talented violinist, Vivaldi was ordained by the Catholic Church. He was given the nickname The Red Priest in reference to his hair color.

LIAM

IN MY DREAM there are soft hands exploring me.

These are the hands of a violinist, incredibly swift and strong and sure. I suck in a breath when they find a decades-old cut on my side. It feels like a lance, the gentle fingertip tracing the scar. They move lower, lower, lower. The backs of delicate knuckles brush against stiff denim, a butterfly beating its wings against a boulder—and breaking it apart.

I roll the warm weight of her beneath me, determined to extract payment. My dick throbs with years of unspent desire. My hands aren't nearly so soft. I'm going to rip her silk-flutter skin the way I'm grabbing her, holding her, using her, but I can't make myself stop.

It's a dream; I don't have to stop.

I press my face into her hair, breathing in the sun-drenched strands. Her skin feels impossibly smooth against my cheek, beneath my lips. I lick her to see if she tastes as sweet. Like the velvet skin of a peach, holding such treasure inside.

The curve of her neck and the place it joins her shoulder. That's where I bite down, reveling in the squeak of sound she makes, the way she stiffens beneath my thighs. Afraid. Afraid. Afraid. She should be scared of me. It would take so little force to break the skin. I must be careful. Even in my dream, I can't hurt her.

I turn my attention lower, to the slope of her breast. The faint memory of black ruffles threatens the edges of my mind… but there is no silk here. There's only a thin T-shirt, and the warning bells recede. My tongue finds her nipple, teasing until it becomes hard enough to bite through the fabric. I've never been tame.

Even when I stand in a suit, in a roomful of a hundred other people, I'm a wild animal wearing clothes. The fact that I choose not to rage and rip and roar does not change who I am.

During sex my base nature reveals fully.

I close my lips around her breast, sucking her through the cotton. My hand plays with her other nipple, which is already hard; it wants my attention there, my mouth.

"Oh God," someone moans, but I must have imagined that.

I find the hem of her shirt and lift until her breasts are exposed to the cool night air. I nuzzle them from underneath, where a deep warmth permeates her skin. And then higher, to her nipple. This is her punishment for touching me, from waking me from hibernation.

She tastes so goddamn sweet. Like sunshine made flesh.

One of my knees nudges her legs apart. My hips settle against hers in an ages-old formation. There's a warm notch for my cock. Even through her panties and my jeans, I can feel the cradle of her body. It's the perfect place to settle while I kiss her breasts.

Forever. That's how long I could remain here, feeling her warmth, petting her softness while she writhes in helpless welcome. While she makes little sounds.

Her hips move against me, hesitant and hungry.

"That's right," I mutter against her nipple, licking in approval. "Make yourself ready for me. I'm so fucking hard right now. I need you soft and ready."

If she isn't, I could hurt her—bruise her secret muscles or tear her tender folds. I clasp her hip and hitch her against me to show her the rhythm. When she comes, her tight little body will clench and release liquid that will ease the way.

She isn't a hot shower and the jerk of my fist. Once I get my cock inside her, I'm going to stay there for a long time. Even when I break her little hymen, I'm going to slide through the blood and the arousal. When I come, I'm going to keep fucking her, the salt enough to sting any break in her skin. Even that wouldn't be enough to make me stop.

Those inquisitive little hands grasp my side, my back, struggling to hold on as the climax rises up. My cock throbs in desperation, feeling the gush of liquid heat. She cries out, and I capture the sound in my mouth, sliding my tongue against hers.

She comes in exquisite little pulses, legs clamping around my body, moaning into my mouth, vibrations I can feel down to my soul. Her body collapses back against the sheets, legs splayed open, arms beside her head. She's never been more beautiful.

"Don't stop now," Dream Samantha says.

Why does she think I would stop? My cock is

hard enough to split in half, made of marble, brought to the breaking point. She's soft and ready for me.

I reach to shove down my jeans. There's no time for anything else; I push aside the wet fabric of her panties. A small pile of curls and slick flesh. Heat races chills along my spine. I press the head of my cock to her—and push push push.

A short, muffled scream of pain pierces the air.

SAMANTHA

LIAM STOPS MOVING, but it does not quiet the chaos. The pulse beating in my ears, the ache in my breasts. The throbbing between my legs. I shouldn't have made a sound. I tried to be quiet. Everyone knows the first time will hurt, but it took me by surprise—both the flash of pain and the fullness. God, the fullness. It's like having a club inside me. Or maybe the curved head of a violin. Something that most definitely does not fit.

"You're not a dream," Liam says, his voice thick as honey.

"A dream?" I say faintly. My legs are spread wide, his body shoving inside me, and he thinks I might not be real. I have the sudden wild urge to giggle—wholly inappropriate. The words *a condom is mandatory* float through my mind. Preposterous, things like practicality, in the face of his wild animal need.

This is nothing planned or careful. This is two animals mating in the jungle. There is no place for latex here.

"I thought—" He makes a low sound of grief. "You're so beautiful and warm. And wet. Samantha, you need to stop clenching like that. It makes me—"

"I'm sorry," I say on a breathless laugh. I'm on the other side of the looking glass now, my old life strange and boring in light of the terrifying wonder before me. "I'm not doing it on purpose."

One thrust of his hips and he pushes in another inch.

I won't survive it. "How much more?"

"I'm not fucking you," he says, unsteady, but there's no conviction in his voice. How can there be when he forces himself another inch?

He's a large man, but I never worried that he wouldn't fit inside me. Men and women perform this act every day. Surely I can figure it out. The theory is nothing more than a smooth water's surface—a mirage replaced with sudden violence by the reality of him. His shoulders loom above me. His muscular thighs hold mine open as wide as they can go. And his cock burrows deeper into my body.

This is everything I've ever wanted, and now that it's here, I can't take it. My body refuses. I wriggle instinctively, trying to get away, to find relief, and he clasps my shoulders in an impossible grip. "No, don't," he gasps, green eyes hazy. "Don't move. Not like that."

"Hurts," I say, barely able to squeeze out the word.

"Sorry. Sorry." He drops his head to taste my shoulder in an openmouthed kiss. "I need to get off you, to stop touching you. To stop fucking you. I'm sorry."

He doesn't stop.

His hips pull away only long enough to let cool air soothe my tender skin. Then he pushes back inside with a grunt. I might as well try to stop a boulder rolling down a mountain, picking up speed as it goes. And I don't want him to stop, not really. It's only that I want this terrible pressure to ease. It makes me pant and writhe.

I don't know whether he's exceptionally large or I'm exceptionally small. Maybe both. It would be only right that we would be mismatched this way, when everything else about us is also wrong. We are not meant to be together; it's only the force of our wills that makes it work.

"No, no," he mutters to himself, fighting it even as he fucks me, thrusting deep inside me, going slow enough that I feel every ounce of friction against my intimate walls. His eyes are wild and angry and somehow frightened. "Make me stop," he says.

I press a kiss to the only part of him I can reach—the bulge of his pecs.

He flinches beneath my lips.

My chest aches with something that has nothing to do with his cock. I'm hurting for the man who thought I'd leave for my tour with a cheerful goodbye and never come back. For the man who thought that would be best for me, as if he's been nothing but a vending machine, a place where I got safety and comfort without ever caring about him in return.

"It's okay," I whisper. "I want this. I want you."

With a groan he thrusts hard inside me. I can only close my eyes, tears leaking down my cheeks. Thank God it's too dark for him to see. He's not looking anyway; his head is down, hips moving swift and fierce. His shout is both masculine power and utter surrender. His body turns taut, straining against me, pushing me into the mattress so hard I can't breathe.

A sense of victory expands in my chest. It's like we climbed the tallest mountain or fought an entire army. That's what we did together, and I stroke his head, feeling the impossible softness as his muscled body weighs me down.

He stirs in slow degrees, his hips moving experimentally, his cock nudging me in an intimate place. I wait for him to pull away. He'll probably leave the bed now. I have no illusions about his reaction to this. I'm the one who started touching him, knowing it would lead to sex. I'm the one who made the overture. He's the one who will retreat.

Except he doesn't leave my body. Instead he thrusts back inside, as if we're still having sex. As if he didn't just flex and spurt warm liquid into my body.

"What are you doing?" I whisper.

"Losing," he says.

"But didn't we just—"

"One time isn't enough," he says, his tone dark with promise.

It sounds like a threat, except the large pulses of cum smooth the way for his cock. They give me a sense of warmth that wasn't there before. Then he shifts his angle slightly, and his cock finds a place inside me that makes me arch and cry out.

"Wait," I say, but he doesn't wait. He does it again, finding the place with a carnal knowledge. How can he know my body better than I do? My secret muscles clench helplessly around him, and he answers with a flex of his cock.

He fucks me with a wealth of patience, pulling pleasure out of my body so long and hard that every muscle hurts, thrusting inside me long enough that I feel myself turn raw. I know what he wants from me, but it's too much.

"I can't," I say in broken sobs, desperate enough to beg.

"You can," he says, his voice a velvet murmur.

His thumb reaches down to press my clit, and I flinch in the few precious moments before the climax overtakes me, clamping down on every muscle, squeezing my lungs, tightening my sex around something too large to fit.

His groan sounds like pain. Like a small and welcome death.

He collapses on me for a second time, and I think to myself, *We've done it. Finally.* Except his cock stirs inside me, and I realize I did not understand the size of this mountain. I did not know the strength of this army.

"Again," he demands, tender and inexorable.

CHAPTER TWENTY-SIX

Stravinsky's ballet The Rite of Spring *was so original and provoking that during its 1913 premier it caused protest and violence from the audience.*

LIAM

"WHAT THE FUCK is this?"

The words rip through the air, tearing me out of sleep.

Elijah stands in the doorway, surveying our naked bodies with a mixture of shock and fury. He looks ready to kill me. I pull on my jeans, so that at least I can die with some dignity.

"Let's take this outside," I say as Samantha stirs in the bed.

"No, you can explain what the fuck you were doing to Samantha Brooks, the child you're responsible for, practically your daughter, right fucking here."

I don't flinch, but it's a close thing. "You don't know what you're talking about."

"Oh really. Did you put your dick in her?"

Josh appears behind him in the hallway, looking almost amused, the bastard. "Are we going to have the birds-and-the-bees talk?"

"You knew about this?" Elijah says, incredulous.

"I figured he was teaching her safe sex."

Elijah lets out a growl. He's always been the one with the most normal sense of morality, between the three of us. "I thought you were better than this," he says softly.

"I'm not," I say because he doesn't need any fucking illusions.

Samantha pulls herself out of bed, fully awake now. "Hey, can you stop talking about me like I'm not part of this? I'm an adult now. I get to make these decisions for myself."

She's using the pink sheet to cover herself, but in the sunbreak it's practically translucent. With a growl I push her behind me. Elijah lets out a snort. "Oh, now you're worried about someone seeing her? After you fucked her?"

"Well, we can see why," Josh says, his tone appreciative. "Look at her with that just-got-fucked hair and whisker burn on her shoulders. Someone's all grown-up."

Red colors my vision, and my control snaps. I launch myself at my brother, throwing a punch that sends him careening into the wall. It leaves me open for a split second—a second that Elijah uses to land a fist in my gut. I absorb the blow with a quiet *oomph,* stepping back from the force. Samantha grabs my arm, which is raised to hit back.

"No," she cries, and the sound cuts through the haze of shame and fury.

"Christ," I say, glaring at Josh. I want another go at him.

"Please," she says, tear tracks glistening on her cheeks. "Don't fight."

"Why the fuck not?" Elijah says, muscles straining as Josh holds him back.

"Because I won't be the reason you hurt each other," Samantha says, her voice trembling. "If you want to punch each other, you'll have to come up with another reason."

She stands there with her chin held high, a sheet wrapped around her slender body. She weighs a hundred pounds of nothing, but she looks like she can stop a war. That's what she's doing, with nothing more than the force of her will.

If there was ever a piece of my heart held back, a part of me that wasn't fully in love with her, it's gone now. She's a warrior. A goddess. I want to fall at her feet in supplication. Now I understand why knights would kneel before their queen and bow their heads. It's the only position that makes sense for a man in the presence of such a woman.

"I love our family reunions," Josh says with a quicksilver grin.

Elijah lets out a low growl that I can empathize with. I wouldn't want to be held back from a fight, either. And I can't even argue his point. I deserve to be beaten. I deserve to be locked in a closet, thrown down a well. I've always deserved it.

"Go," she says, her head held high. "I love that you care about me this much, and I know that because of a messed-up childhood, this may be the only way you know how to show it. But I'm a grown woman. You don't get to dictate who I sleep with. And I'm asking you to leave."

Only Elijah looks at all chastened by the words. Josh gives an irreverent little salute before heading down the hallway. I'm the only one left, and I turn to face her.

"Samantha, I'm sorry. I shouldn't have—"

"You too," she says softly, heartbreak lending her brown eyes an almost rust-colored red. "You're the worst one, about to apologize for taking my virginity not even a full day after you did it. I deserve better than that. If you want to get back into bed, to try to find some peace and joy together, then you can stay. But if you want to apologize for wanting me, you can leave."

I swallow hard, but there's only one thing I can do.

My feet suddenly weigh a thousand tons. My head swims with the certainty that I will regret this moment until my final day. And my heart beats with a terrible truth, that I can't possibly stay in this room. Josh was wrong when he said I was still holding on to that baby bird in the closet. I have to let her go. And so I walk out of the room, my expression stoic as it slams behind me. We can't be on the same side of the door, not when I'm trapped in hell.

SAMANTHA

I GREW UP without being able to count on my father. Even when Liam North became my guardian, part of me had already learned not to trust grown-ups. They only wanted to tell me what to do, only wanted me to please them. Some things are learned deep in your bones.

I couldn't wait to become an adult so that I

could make my own decisions. Now that I'm here, I realize something was missing in my dreams of adulthood. I can make my own choices; I can choose Liam, but I can't make him choose me. The sky is full of wind and storm; my wings only take me so far.

That's how I find myself playing the Lady Tennant, my own composition of loss and heartbreak. It makes me think of biting cold and lonely nights. I thought I wanted to graduate from high school, to turn eighteen, to play on a tour—when all I really wanted was not to be left behind.

That's what's happening, even if I'm the one walking out the door.

We're not going to be pen pals. I may be an adult now, but Liam still makes the rules. I can't make him write or call or visit me. And I definitely can't make him love me.

The composition ends abruptly, written only in my head.

It felt wrong to give it one last sorrowful note.

It felt final.

Now the true end comes to me, a silvery line that flutters, uncertain. It darts this way and that, caught on some uplifting wind.

The notes rise higher, ending on the auspice

of hope.

Only a few months ago, my bow fell still in the middle of a song. Now it comes to a graceful close at the end of one I wrote myself. Instead of waiting for Liam to react to the silence, I stand and cross the threshold.

He sits at his office, not making any pretense of work. His large flat-screen monitor is dark. The black leather blotter on his desk is empty. The lamp is off.

"Did you like it?" I ask.

"It was the most beautiful thing I've ever heard."

A window behind him provides the only illumination. Moonlight limns his broad shoulders and fair hair. I think more than anything that's happened, *this* is what marks adulthood. Fighting for the life I want.

Fighting for the man I love.

Circling his desk, I come to stand in front of him. His chair is turned slightly so that I can kneel down almost in front of him. The way he did to me a thousand times, a light touch on my knee, looking me in the eyes like I was important to him.

The deep green of his eyes is only a suggestion in the shadows.

I touch my palms to his knees. "You don't want to hear me play in concert?"

"I want it more than life," he says, his voice rough—even rougher when my hands skate on top of his thighs. I already fought for him with music. Now there's a different kind of battle to be waged. "More than I should."

"More than writing letters," I say, a small mocking note.

"We're not—" A sharp indrawn breath as I feel his hardness through his slacks. "We're not going to be pen pals."

I shake my head slowly. "That's not what I want from you anyway."

He moves as if to push me away, only to fall still when I touch the head of his cock. That's when he goes completely still, hissing out a breath. "What you want is impossible."

"Explain it to me," I say, tracing a ridge that circles him. Everything about this is new and exciting. I would enjoy it if there weren't so much on the line.

"I'm not—Oh God, sweetheart. I'm not made for that. All I do is hurt people, all I do is trap them. Starve them. Make them close their eyes and go to sleep."

His words don't make sense on the surface,

but they do on a deep level. I feel them resonate on the same level as my bone-deep certainties. That I'll always be left by a man who doesn't love me. And he's so worried about trapping me that he's determined to leave. We make quite a pair.

"You don't have to protect me anymore," I whisper. "I'm grown-up now."

"You won't ever be old enough, understand? It's not about your age. It's about the fact that I'm responsible for you. I can't let you die."

Maybe it should scare me—that word. *I can't let you die.* Except this is a man who has lived with death as his shadow for so long. I see what it costs him to send men and women into danger. What it costs him to risk his own brothers with every mission.

I find the button to his slacks and work them, clumsy in the dark. And then his zipper. At any moment he might stop me. His breathing saws in and out, audible even though he can run twelve miles a morning barely breaking a sweat. *This* is what's straining him, the hardness of his cock in my hand. It feels softer than I expected. The salt tang of him comes to me in the dark, and I nudge toward him, in search of his desire. My nose bumps his cock first, and a shudder runs through him.

"Samantha," he says on a helpless chant. "Samantha. *Samantha.*"

Blindly I search for him in the dark, my lips landing on some velvet-burn place on him. I send my tongue to feel him, to trace a raised vein. Then I pull back, toward the tip, finding that ridge again, exploring it with my mouth while he pants and groans above me, a benediction in the night.

"Is this okay?" I say, pausing uncertainly.

His hand lands on top of my head, falling down to stroke my hair, to grab it in unruly fistfuls. "It's more than okay. It's incredible. I can't take it. I'm dying."

I might not know what he means except that he did the same thing to me while I played Beethoven's "5 Secrets." Which means I know that dying means he's close—but not there yet. So I lick him again, remembering the rhythm he used between my legs.

His hips push forward in small thrusts, uncontrolled, almost as if he can't stop them. His cock moves through the circle of my fist, the same way he did in the shower.

My lips feel swollen as I pull back, sliding against the soft head of his cock as I speak. "You were angry at me that I kept the Coach Price thing a secret, but how many secrets are you keeping from me?"

"It's my job to keep those secrets."

"Bullshit," I say, punctuating the word with a pump of my fist. The velvet skin moves apart from the hard muscle beneath. "I'm not talking about any of your classified government contracts. I'm talking about you and me and how I came to be in your custody."

He makes a sound of protest—and I don't want to hear him give me more lies, more platitudes. More attempts to soothe his own guilt by telling himself that's what I need from him.

So I press a kiss to the head of his cock, to where the wetness pools into a salty drop. I lick it away from him. And lick again, to find that another one has formed. It's a sensual feast, doing this in the dark, hearing his shuddery breaths.

"You have to stop," he says, his hips pushing harder and harder.

I make my fist tighter around him, working him, making love to him with my hand—it isn't impersonal at all. This is the way I make music with my bow and violin. Every twitch of my fingers, every slight pressure. His ragged breathing and low groans are the music I make.

Heat gathers between my legs, but I force

myself to ignore that. There are more important things at stake than my arousal, the dampness in my sex. The ache in my clit.

"Don't you know how it takes away my power, not to know what happened to my own father, what happened to me? I can't even remember that night. Only that when I woke up, my father was dead and there was a stranger who would take care of me. Don't you see how it's hurting me?"

A low animal sound of pain fills the air, making the hair on the back of my neck rise. He does see it, he does, but he can't do anything except succumb to the physical release. I close my mouth around his cock, catching his climax on my tongue. I swallow, greedy, knowing this might be my only taste. I lave him gently, kiss him, kiss him, soothing him as he comes down in jerks and pants.

Without warning or ceremony, he drags me onto his lap, fingers working quickly at my jeans, finding their way inside to the slick center. I jerk at the intrusion. Too much friction, too fast. "Wait," I whisper.

"Now," he says, unbending.

I try to clamp my legs shut, but it only makes the pressure more intense. "Tell me we can have more than this. Tell me you'll see me on the tour.

Tell me you'll wait for me to come back."

He doesn't tell me any of those things. His silence is answer enough. My body doesn't realize it's lost—the climax builds in pleasure-drenched waves, leaving me panting and sated on the lap of a man who's just turned me away.

His lips brush my forehead, chaste even as my arousal dries on his fingers. "There is no future for you and me. I'm no longer your guardian. You're no longer my ward."

Tears dampen my lashes. "We could make something new."

He pushes me gently off his lap, and I stagger like a deer on my legs for the first time. "You're forgetting something, sweetheart. I don't want that."

Every molecule in my body shouts at me to push him, to shake him, to make him see that we can work. Whether he's trying to protect me or protect himself, the result is the same. I can't make him want this. And I don't think he'll ever really see me as an adult while I live under his roof.

CHAPTER TWENTY-SEVEN

There are two skulls in composer Joseph Haydn's tomb. His head was stolen by phrenologists and a replacement skull was put in his tomb. In 1954, the real skull was restored, but the substitute was not removed.

LIAM

MY HANDS ARE steeped in blood and dirt. I've been working through the obstacle course we use for training for the past five hours, pretending that my life is at stake—because in some ways it is. I set every barrier to its highest point, every weight to its heaviest. I'm still alive, which means we really need to make it harder. Torn muscles ache everywhere in my body. I wipe the sweat and grit from my eyes.

I started this afternoon, and the sun set a little while ago. Footsteps approach from the house. My senses are dulled by pain, which is the point.

"Go the fuck away," I tell Josh. He's come to check on me every hour, offering water and energy bars and once, the use of his pistol. *Finish the fucking job, if that's what you want,* he said. He should have given it to Elijah, who probably wouldn't mind using it.

"I might," comes a feminine voice. *Samantha.* "I have some questions first."

I drag myself into a sitting position, leaning back against a 4x4 staked into the ground. The world tilts wildly until I close my eyes. Something nudges my hand. A bottle of water. I take a swallow, downing half the liquid before I take a breath.

Samantha kneels in front of me, the way I did so often as she played the violin. She holds out something in her hand, her expression solemn. It's a couple of ibuprofens. I stare at the pills, so innocuous and small, so ordinary when the world is shattering. I swallow them down and finish the rest of the water. "Thanks," I say gruffly.

"How did you know my father?" she says, her brown eyes as clear as I've ever seen them in the deepening night. "The real answer this time."

"I wasn't friends with him," I admit. "We hadn't ever met."

She takes a seat a few feet away, her legs crossed. She's wearing jeans and a T-shirt with her high school crest on it—which makes her look like a child. She isn't a child anymore, but that doesn't change what she is to me. Like the bird that fell from the nest before it could fly.

"Go on," she says.

"He was a spy," I say, my voice abrupt. Businesslike. Because this had been my business for so long. "He took money under the table from a few different countries, but mostly Russia. It was my job to identify men like that and then eliminate them. But sometimes we would wait. If they could be useful, we'd keep them around, let them lead us to even bigger targets."

Her eyes are troubled, though she doesn't look particularly surprised. It's as if I'm reminding her of something she already knew. Children are smart, even when they don't know all the facts. They know what's important. "That's how you knew him? You were watching him?"

"Those were my orders, except he started getting too erratic."

She's quiet a moment. "So your team eliminated him?"

"No, sweetheart. I did that."

A flinch. "You were just doing your job."

Even now she wants to make excuses for me. "My orders were to continue to watch him. They wanted to see what happened next. I already knew, and I wasn't going to wait around. So I slipped a little something into his special dark roast coffee beans, the ones he guarded so fucking religiously that no one else could drink it."

Her eyes are wide. She knows what's coming next. "The coffee."

She never drank coffee with me, not once. Only tea. Some part of her recognized the danger, even if she couldn't remember why. "I didn't know that a twelve-year-old little girl liked to sneak a sip of the stuff. Not until I found out she was in the hospital."

Tears fall down her cheeks. "That's why I don't remember."

"They didn't put it together at the time. An old man dying of a heart attack. A young girl who'd seen it, passed out with memory loss from seeing something tragic. By the time anyone thought to investigate, he was cremated."

"Is that why you wanted custody of me?" she says, the words like venom, full of pain. "To make sure no one could run a blood test on me without your permission?"

"Christ. No, Samantha. Any trace would be gone from your system."

"Then why?"

"Because you deserved a hell of a lot better than a traitor for a father and a bastard for a brother." I give a humorless laugh, knocking my head back against the splintery wood. "Do you know what I regret the most? Not killing him. I'm sorry I didn't do it sooner. I had to watch him forget to feed you, forget to clothe you. I saw him leave you at the square in Leningrad while it was snowing, and you weren't even wearing boots—I couldn't call anyone to get you because it would prove he was being surveilled."

She listens to me speak and then gives a brief nod, as if our conversation is concluded. And I suppose it is. This is the only way it could end—with the truth.

SAMANTHA

IN SOME WAYS the information about my father wasn't a surprise. I may not have known the specifics, but I knew what kind of man he was. Loyalty wasn't in his vocabulary. And if I had thought more about it—the money that would come and go. The way he'd buy me a new dress to attend a fancy dinner one week and then leave the pantry empty the next. Alistair Brooks was a desperate man. And I was his desperate daughter, so eager to believe that someone cared about me that I invented stories. If only I could play violin well enough, if I followed the rules hard enough. If I wanted it bad enough, there would be a father to love me.

Growing up isn't about learning something new. It's about unlearning the fairy tales you believe as a child. Elijah offered to take me away from here, but I won't put that between the brothers. Instead I call a cab and pack a single carry-on suitcase. A flight leaves Austin in a few hours that will take me to Chicago, and then on to Tanglewood. I can start my new life there, a little earlier than I had planned. I'm ready.

I put my suitcase in the car and step into the back of the cab. The front door opens, and Liam strides toward me. *Don't ask me to stay,* I beg him silently. I'm not sure I can say no. It's not because I stopped loving him. I think I love him even more now, somehow, seeing him battered and broken against the obstacle course he built himself, beating himself against his own guilt. But he will never see me as a grown woman while I stay here. He will never accept me as an equal while I remain in his custody, if only in body and not spirit.

The only choice is to leave, which means it's not really a choice at all.

His silhouette breaks from the house, and I

realize he's holding the violin. The Stradivarius. I hadn't brought it with me. There are violins everywhere, and societies and museums would be happy to loan me a great one. It wouldn't equal the Lady Tennant, but nothing would.

"Why did you leave it behind?" he asks, his voice hoarse.

"I wasn't sure you'd want me to have it. After everything that happened."

His green eyes are lighter than I've ever seen them, almost see-through. This is the most he's ever shown me of him—his past, his emotion. All it took was for me to leave.

"Bullshit," he says.

"Fine. Maybe I wasn't sure I still wanted it. After everything that happened."

"Take it. That is, if you want to play this violin, then I want you to have it."

I swallow hard and take the case, my fingers brushing his on the wooden handle.

"And if you ever need me—" His voice breaks.

"I know where to find you," I finish for him.

He shuts the door and slaps the top of the cab so we move forward. I watch my home disappear through my tears. Only when we get to the airport do I realize that it's Josh driving the cab.

"What the hell?" I say as he steps out to squint at a parking meter.

"Do you have a quarter?" he says, digging through his pocket.

With an exasperated sigh I reach into my jeans and find a dollar bill. He plucks it out of my hands. "Thanks. You have now officially hired North Security as your personal bodyguard."

I cross my arms. "Pretty sure that's not legally binding."

"And I'm pretty sure Liam North would shit a brick before he ever let you leave without adequate protection. The guy in the Crown Vic may be dead, but someone else ordered the hit. You're not safe until we neutralize them for good."

A rush of emotion wells in my throat. I know I need to leave Liam, but it hurts worse than anything I can imagine. I could turn Lady Tennant into firewood, and it still wouldn't break my heart as much as this. A sob escapes me, and Josh's face blurs into a thousand pointillism dots. Through the tears, I see him open his arms. I let him hold me as I break apart. He has the same build as Liam, the same coloring, and I feel close to the man I love—and so far away I'm not sure we'll ever be able to cross the distance.

LIAM

I SIT IN the armchair in my office, the fire blazing. It can't penetrate the chill. Samantha took any warmth from the house, and I don't expect it to return.

That doesn't absolve me of my responsibility where she's concerned.

I should probably feel guilty about defiling a priceless violin with a micro-tracking device, but there is nothing I won't do to keep her safe.

Elijah enters the room, his face implacable. He wants to kick my ass, but it's a testament to how terrible I look that he doesn't bother.

"You're a bastard," he says instead, no heat in his voice.

"Are you more angry that I failed in protecting Samantha—or that I failed in protecting you?" I enlisted the day I turned eighteen, leaving my brothers behind. Josh was old enough to defend himself by then, at least. Elijah had no such power. It took years before I had the money and the strength to return home to get him out of there.

"You didn't fail," he says. "That's not giving Samantha enough credit."

No, she became a strong woman with fierce loyalty. No thanks to me. I don't expect I'll ever get to touch her again. Won't get to see her except from afar. But I can damn well protect her. "A drug lord?"

A humorless smile. "That was an unexpected detour."

"Christ, Elijah."

"We found the target and confirmed his identity."

I flip through the pages in a manila folder, proof that one Kimberly Cox never actually existed. She has a convincing portfolio of freelance articles, an apartment in Brooklyn, a 401K. She had a contract with *Classical Notes* to interview the performers on tour.

Except that she's not a real person.

The woman who came to our house that day was a fraud.

"Did he make you?" I ask.

"Negative, but he knows someone's after him."

A few months ago I heard whispers that Alistair Brooks survived the assassination.

I sent the Red Team to find out if the whispers were true. And then a reporter shows up asking questions about her background. Quite a coincidence. That had been enough to make me concerned. I stepped up her security detail quietly, making sure one of the men was always nearby.

Josh will keep her safe while I find the traitorous fucker and finish the job.

She'll be safe once and for all—and she won't ever have to know that the man who ordered the hit was her father.

Thank You for Reading

Thank you so much for reading OVERTURE!

I hope you love Liam and Samantha. Find out what happens when Samantha goes on tour in CONCERTO, and Liam learns he can't live without her.

The spotlight lands on Samantha Brooks. Years of practice build to the opening night of a global tour. She plays her heart out, but there are darker forces underneath the stage.

There are eyes watching from the wings.

Liam North fights to keep her safe with every weapon he owns. She's his greatest pride—and his greatest weakness. The danger comes from somewhere no one expected. Betrayal threatens to destroy everything he's built. His business. His family. His life.

When the curtain falls, only one of them will be left standing.

CONCERTO is available from bookstores now!

And you can read Hugo and Bea's story right

now! Find out what happens when a seductive and jaded male escort shows up at the penthouse of an innocent heiress…

> "A sensual feast! Escort is extraordinary—delicious, passionate, dreamily sexy and utterly romantic! One of my favorite books of the year and I will be recommending it to everyone!"
>
> —#1 NYT Bestselling author
> Lauren Blakely

Turn the page for an excerpt from CONCERTO…

Excerpt from Concerto

Her breath catches. "I missed you."

The words tumble out of her mouth, as if she can't hold them back. My heart clenches, a painful squeeze that reminds me of every second I've been apart from her.

One day I had been a man with a death wish—and the next I was responsible for a twelve-year-old girl. And then she grew up into a beautiful woman. At every turn she's been a surprise.

I touch my fingers to her temple and stroke her cheek. "If there's one thing I've learned in life it's that everything will change. Don't worry about your future. Do this because you love it, right now. Play. Compose. Perform. Sometimes all you have is right now."

My hand trails down her jaw, until the backs of my fingers rest against her throat. Her vocal cords vibrate as she speaks. Ripples of pleasure and pain resound through my body.

"I'm not performing right now," she whispers.

I have her tucked into the ivy, as deep as she can go. I'm blocking her with my body—keeping her within reach, keeping everyone else away. It's the only way I've ever been able to breathe.

A knot forms in my throat. "What do you want?"

Right now. The words move between us like the cool night breeze.

It shouldn't be possible for her to live up to the image in my head, the perfection that I've been imagining every goddamn night. Except it doesn't even do her justice.

She's living breathing perfection.

Somehow, I'm leaning close. Is it only me who wants this? Her breath brushes over my lips. "Right now, I want this," she whispers, and then she closes the centimeters between us.

Four weeks. That's how long I've been apart from her.

It might as well have been four years. A lifetime of silence. The moment her lips touch mine I'm suffused with music, thousands of notes that she's played for me, a million heartbeats.

By the time she pulls back I'm breathing hard. I can run a marathon barely breaking a sweat. Being near this woman is enough to break my body into pieces.

"Right now," I say, my voice unsteady.

"That's all we have." Her eyes search mine. "Or is there more?"

"You need to get back. They'll be waiting for you."

Disappointment darkens her pretty face. "Yeah, and somehow I was late. I swear my invitation didn't say anything about a cocktail hour before dinner. God, I wonder if they did that on purpose. Harry said they want us to have drama so we get more press."

"You're a world-class musician, Samantha. They can go to hell. Besides, we have bigger problems to worry about. Like the fact that you're still in danger."

A soft intake of breath. "How do you know?"

Because I tortured a man until he pissed himself. That's something she doesn't need to know. "It doesn't matter. The intelligence is good. That's the important part. So no going outside without Josh. I'm going to have a talk with him."

"Liam," she whispers. "Why are they doing this?"

"Because I have a responsibility to you. They know that. So they'll use you to draw me out. You would be bait, to get revenge on almost killing your father."

A notch forms between her eyebrows. "Who would avenge him?"

"He would. Your father isn't dead, Samantha."

A ripple of shock moves through her body. I wish I could shield her from it, but I take a step back instead. She's going to face this particular truth on her own. How can I help her when I'm the reason he should have died? When I'm the reason he's still alive?

"You're wrong," she says, her voice rough.

"I thought that fucker was sent to kill you, but you know what I think now? He was sent to kidnap you. You would be bait to bring me out of hiding."

Her eyes shine with unshed tears. "I don't understand."

Ancient pieces of my heart rattle, where ordinary human emotion would usually go. I want to take away all of her worries. I want to kill her father the way I should have years ago. Until six months ago I believed I had succeeded. I left a young girl alone in the world, and that guilt led me to take custody of her. It was a terrible domino effect—her father's duplicity, my assassination of him, my guardianship of Samantha.

"Understand this," I tell her. "Your father is

not a good man."

She shakes her head, which isn't to disagree. It's more about being overwhelmed. "You know what? Fine. I believe you wouldn't have tried to kill him without cause. That still doesn't explain why you're here. Isn't that what they want? Luring you out?"

"I can take care of myself."

A snort. "Yes, the powerful Liam North doesn't need anyone."

"I came to warn you. To make sure you understand the stakes."

"Oh, I understand them." She sounds a little sad. Mostly resigned. "I'm starting to think you have a hero complex. You don't want to be with me? Then don't worry about my life."

That's the last thing she says to me before returning to the restaurant.

A hero complex? That's ironic, considering I've never been anyone's hero. Definitely not Samantha's. That's something she's going to find out before this is over. Then again, part of her may already know. I think she remembers more than she wants to admit.

Excerpt from Escort

THERE ARE ASS men and there are breast men. I can appreciate a beautiful ass or a nice rack. The blood in my veins is red, after all. But what I really am, what drives me absolutely crazy, what seems obscene even though women walk around with them in full view, are freckles. There's something about them, the way they scatter over skin, the knowledge of the other places they must cover, that makes me hard as a rock. I have this primal instinct to map the constellations on Bea's body.

Her black dress covers more than it shows. The fabric reveals an hourglass figure that I would love to run my hands along, but we aren't close to that. And above the high neckline, that's where the freckles begin. Only a shade darker than her natural skin color, which is pale.

Pale enough to turn a charming pink whenever she's nervous.

"Thank you for coming," she says, pink all the

way from the point of her nose to her neck. I would bet tonight's entire fee, which is sizable, that the pink extends across her breasts.

Everything about her is closed, her legs pressed together where she perches on the armchair, her lips clamped shut as if to keep herself from saying more. In contrast I'm a study in openness, my ankle slung over my knee, arm stretched across the top of the sofa.

"It's my pleasure," I assure her. "I'm touched that you trust me in your home."

She glances around, as if considering for the first time that she ought not have invited me inside. "We could get a room downstairs, maybe. Unless they're sold out."

"I'd rather be where you're most comfortable."

She gives a small laugh of embarrassment. "I'm not sure I'm capable of being comfortable."

"Shall we call down for dinner?" I offer, mostly because the opportunity to eat and drink and breathe will help soothe her. But also because it will give me more time with her, this woman who may hold the answers to my long-held questions.

"No, thank you."

"We could go out. I know a lovely bistro not two blocks away."

She shakes her head, almost stricken. "No."

Such refusal, this one has. Such determination.

Her eyes are wary, watching as I stroke the brocade fabric of the sofa leisurely. It's almost like she expects me to lunge at her, to rip her clothes away without any discussion. Of course, I would most enjoy that, if I thought she wanted me to do it.

My curiosity is a living, breathing presence in the room. I want to unravel her secrets. Why does the idea of leaving make her anxiety spike like a tangible blaze in the air?

I decide to go for frankness. "You're a lovely woman, Bea. It would be an honor to spend the evening with you, but I have to be honest. I don't usually work for clients as young as you."

A blink. "You don't?"

One shoulder lifts. "The CEO of a multinational corporation who realizes she's spent more time on work than building a social life. A divorcee who wants to experience pleasure without resentment. They are the usual, but I have a feeling those don't quite apply to you."

"Not exactly," she says, cheeks almost cherry pink.

The cat has found a perch on top of an old

roll-top desk, her yellow eyes trained on me. I don't mind one female looking at me. Don't mind two. To be honest I have a bit of the exhibitionist in me, one of the many reasons I'm in the perfect profession. I know without looking that my shoes are perfectly shined, my bespoke suit conforming effortlessly to my body. Bea's green gaze, both nervous and curious, is the best foreplay I could want.

"I don't need to know what led you to call me, certainly not the details of your circumstances, but it would help if I knew what you expect out of our evening."

"Oh God," she says on a groan. "I'm screwing this up, aren't I? There's probably a secret handshake or something and I don't know it. You must think I'm insane."

I shake my head, slow and slight. "No secret handshake, I promise. There's only you and me, having a conversation about pleasure."

The word seems to take her aback. "Pleasure?"

"That's the nature of my business, yes." My body tightens, because it would be pleasure indeed to touch this woman. To kiss her. To make her moan for me.

Although I might have to rethink that plan, because the word *pleasure* might as well have been *medieval torture* based on the way Bea looks at me. "I thought we were going to have sex."

She sounds so forlorn it could break my heart.

Instead I laugh, a small huff of breath, because I can't afford to have a heart.

"Sex," I say, standing to full height, circling the scuffed oriental coffee table, standing behind her chair. "And pleasure. Pleasure and sex. They're interchangeable."

I brush my knuckles over the side of her neck, a demonstration. Her wild curls tickle my skin.

It's provocative, this. If she had agreed to dinner I would have started with small touches, a glance of my palm against the small of her back as I pulled out her chair, holding her hand while we talked over a glass of wine. Perhaps being so bold as to run a finger along the inside of hers, where it's more sensitive. She would shiver; her gaze would meet mine.

There's an order to these things. You can move fast or slow, but there's still an order.

"We can skip the pleasure part," she says, her voice high, her breathing faster. Her chest rises and falls in the black dress, made all the more alluring by how much it covers. She's a mystery. The black sky in the city. I have to work to see her secrets.

"No," I chide gently. "We focus on the pleasure. That's the point."

"What if—" Her breath catches as I drop the back of my hand over her collarbone, a reverse caress. That's what one does for a skittish creature like her. "What if I have a different point?"

"And what point would that be, my sweet Bea?"

"I want to lose my virginity," she says, so fast it comes out as a single word.

Want to read more? ESCORT is available now on Amazon, Barnes & Noble, Apple Books, and Kobo.

Books by Skye Warren

Endgame trilogy & more books in Tanglewood

The Pawn

The Knight

The Castle

The King

The Queen

Escort

Survival of the Richest

The Evolution of Man

A Modern Fairy Tale Duet

Beauty and the Professor

Falling for the Beast

Chicago Underground series

Rough

Hard

Fierce

Wild

Dirty

Secret

Sweet

Deep

Stripped series

Tough Love

Love the Way You Lie

Better When It Hurts

Even Better

Pretty When You Cry

Caught for Christmas

Hold You Against Me

To the Ends of the Earth

For a complete listing of Skye Warren books, visit

www.skyewarren.com/books

About the Author

Skye Warren is the New York Times bestselling author of dangerous romance such as the Endgame trilogy. Her books have been featured in Jezebel, Buzzfeed, USA Today Happily Ever After, Glamour, and Elle Magazine. She makes her home in Texas with her loving family, sweet dogs, and evil cat.

Sign up for Skye's newsletter:

www.skyewarren.com/newsletter

Like Skye Warren on Facebook:

facebook.com/skyewarren

Join Skye Warren's Dark Room reader group:

skyewarren.com/darkroom

Follow Skye Warren on Instagram:

instagram.com/skyewarrenbooks

Visit Skye's website for her current booklist:

www.skyewarren.com

COPYRIGHT

Print Edition
Cover design by Book Beautiful
Formatted by BB eBooks

CPSIA information can be obtained
at www.ICGtesting.com
Printed in the USA
LVHW031632291019
635704LV00004B/828/P